HUTCHINS CREEK CACHE

Deborah Garner

Cranberry Cove Press

Hutchins Creek Cache
by Deborah Garner

First Printing – September 2016
ISBN: 978-0-9960449-6-7

Printed in the U.S.A.

Also by Deborah Garner

Above the Bridge
The Moonglow Café
Three Silver Doves
Cranberry Bluff
Mistletoe at Moonglow
A Flair for Chardonnay

To Jay Garner

CHAPTER ONE

Long billows of steam puffed upward, fluid shapes against a stunning blue sky. Each sudden burst painted a new image above the sturdy steel engine below: cotton candy, an elephant, a favorite childhood blanket, down feathers from a duckling.

Had she not been so exhausted, Paige could have watched the ever-changing shapes for hours. She dragged her suitcase to a wooden bench next to the train station's ticket window. Sitting down, she slouched back against the wall and watched new sculptures of steam float upward: a rabbit's cottontail, the concave sail of a boat, an umbrella carried off by the wind.

From the window of the train, she'd seen only pine trees and granite cliffs as they'd pulled into the station. Although she'd known the small town of Hutchins Creek was nestled among those trees, it hadn't been visible through the mountain landscape.

"Ms. MacKenzie?"

The voice mixed with the shrill, unexpected blast of the train's whistle, both incongruous with the peaceful surroundings.

"Yes?" Paige answered. "I'm sorry. I could barely hear you above the train." She sized him up. He was at least seventy, dressed in jeans, a faded red shirt and a tan fisherman's bucket hat. A bolo tie added a touch of eccentricity to his outfit.

"Happens all the time," he said. "Can't compete with those whistles. I'm Henry Sanders. Rose sent me down to pick you up." He extended his arm, which Paige mistook for an attempted handshake. As he grabbed the handle of her suitcase, she brushed her hand down the right leg of her jeans, as if that had been her intent all along.

"Rosemary Hutchins?" Paige asked. She stood up and pulled the strap of her tote bag over her shoulder, letting it rest against her side.

Henry nodded, and pointed Paige toward an old Ford that was at least three decades old.

"Yes, indeed," Henry said. "She's just 'Rose' to us around these parts, but everywhere else she's Rosemary Hutchins, great-granddaughter of Jed Hutchins. He founded Hutchins Creek."

Paige followed Henry to the car. As he lifted the trunk lid, metal hinges squeaked. He placed Paige's suitcase inside, and Paige winced when the lid grated again as he slammed it shut.

Henry opened the passenger door for Paige, tipping the floppy brim of his hat as she climbed in. Closing the door, he circled around to the driver's side and slid behind the wheel.

"Yep, good old Jed Hutchins, rest his soul," Henry continued, "and the souls of all the other Hutchins men, too, every last one of 'em rascals." A faint smile crossed Henry's face.

"Almost sounds like you knew them all," Paige said. She searched for a seatbelt, but found none.

"Knew them all?" Henry repeated. "Do I look like I'm a hundred and fifty years old? Don't answer that! That's what you call a rhetorical question. But I've heard the stories. We all have. Those Hutchins boys are legendary."

Paige smiled and settled into her seat, then shifted quickly when a spring inside the upholstery poked her back.

"Watch out for that seat cushion," Henry said, a moment too late. "It'll get you every time. Keep meaning to fix it. Poor Lulu's gettin' old."

"Lulu?" Paige twisted sideways and found a comfortable spot for her shoulder. Cautiously, she leaned against the seat.

"This here car," Henry said. He reached forward and patted the top of the dashboard affectionately. "Bought her in '78, and she's never let me down."

"Reliability is a great feature," Paige said, grasping for a reply. She jumped as the glove compartment fell open when Henry turned the key in the ignition.

"Gotta get that repaired," Henry said. "I keep meaning to tie that thing shut until then." He reached in front of Paige and closed the small storage area, slamming it three times before the latch caught.

Paige rested against the car's seatback again, but avoided the upholstery spring as best she could while Henry pulled out of the parking lot. He turned left and headed immediately up a hill, following a relatively well-maintained road, barring a few potholes. Twice Paige caught the glove compartment's door as it fell open. Finally, she placed one hand over it, and discovered a double advantage: the door stayed closed, and she kept her balance.

"Steep roads around here," Paige commented.

"Nothin' but," Henry said. "If you want flat roads, you're in the wrong town. Yes, sir – I mean ma'am – we leave flatness to Durango and Denver and any other place where the altitude stays the same for at least twenty feet at a stretch. You won't find anywhere like that in Hutchins Creek."

Paige smiled, but said nothing, instead taking in the tall evergreens on either side of the road. Sunlight filtered between the trees like bright mist, and the scent of pine filled the clean, fresh air. Hutchins Creek offered a completely different environment from that of her last assignment. Writing about the mineral springs in Tres Palomas, New Mexico, had been enchanting in a southwestern way, from the warm desert landscape to the mouthwatering cuisine. But the crisp mountain air and late summer foliage that surrounded her now promised a different experience.

Three minutes and two more left turns brought reliable Lulu to the front curb of the Hutchins Creek Inn, a modest western structure with a brick walkway leading to the front door. Set on a street that appeared to randomly mix commercial properties with residential, it was an attractive building surrounded by well-maintained gardens. A quaint gazebo sat in one corner of the front yard under a cluster of quaking aspens.

Had it not been for the unexpected figure on the front porch of the inn, Paige would have been tempted to check in and head straight for the gazebo, which promised to be a perfect writing spot. Instead, tossing a rushed mix of "thank you!" and "excuse me!" to Henry, she jumped out of the car and dashed up the brick walkway, landing in the arms of her favorite Jackson Hole cowboy. Equally excited, Jake Norris lifted Paige off the ground and swung her around in a circle before setting her back down.

"Jake! What are you doing here already? You weren't supposed to come in until tomorrow!"

Paige fought to catch her breath. The three months in New York since her last assignment had diminished her tolerance for high altitudes. Or was it the excitement of seeing Jake that had her fighting for air? Aside from the fact they hadn't seen each other for months, this was also the first time they'd planned ahead to be together while she was on assignment. That alone had kept Paige's nerves twisted over the previous few weeks.

"I finished up the ranch business early. I couldn't wait to see you," Jake said, stepping back, but holding on to both of her hands. "You look great."

"So do you," Paige said. Heat crept up her neck. It was true; he looked as handsome as he always did whenever their schedules allowed them time together. He wore western boots, well-fitting jeans, and a favorite plaid shirt that perfectly matched his blue eyes, attire like he'd worn when she first met him almost a year ago. He even had a familiar silver belt buckle on, one edged with just a trace of gold.

Of course, he had the advantage, arriving early. She didn't need a mirror to know her auburn hair was a mess from the train ride, and she was still weary from traveling from New York the day before. Had she even put make up on that morning? She couldn't remember. She would have swiped a bit of mascara over her eyelashes and brushed some blush on her cheeks if she'd known Jake was going to be greeting her. Not that she needed blush at the moment, she realized. Her cheeks were certain to be red.

"I do hate to interrupt this tender moment."

"Oh," Paige exclaimed, realizing Henry had walked up beside her, bringing her belongings from the car: one suitcase and one backpack that served as an overnight bag.

"I'm sorry, Henry," Paige said. "This is Jake Norris." She watched as Henry set the bags down and nodded to Jake, who returned the gesture.

"Yeah, we met yesterday," Henry said.

"Ah, I see…" Paige looked between the two men, silently accusing them of being conspirators. Her eyes settled back on Henry. "Did you pick Jake up at the station yesterday? I guess you didn't want to spoil his surprise by telling me. I understand."

"Thanks, but you're giving me too much credit there," Henry said. "I didn't give him a ride. He drove in all on his own. I met him when I stopped by to bring Rose some magazines I was finished with."

"You missed a great train ride, then," Paige said, turning her attention back to Jake. "Did you drive all the way here from Wyoming?"

Jake laughed. "Yes, I did, dropped off some paperwork in Rock Springs on the way down. And 'all the way' isn't that far, since Colorado and Wyoming border each other, except Jackson is at the north end of one state, and you ended up near the south end of the other."

"Well, I don't have complete say over these assignments," Paige said in her defense.

It was true. Her editor, Susan, gave her a lot of leeway when it came to proposing articles for *The Manhattan Post*, but Susan still had final say. This time the old railroad history of the Durango area had won out over an article Paige initially pitched on haunted hotels that were farther north. Still, the train ride up from Durango had convinced her that they'd been right to go with railroads. There was something appealing, even romantic, about the old steam trains.

"I'm heading out now," Henry said. "It was a pleasure meeting you, Ms. MacKenzie. I'm sure I'll see you again during your stay."

"I hope so," Paige said. "Thanks for the ride. And for introducing me to Lulu." She returned Henry's wave and then faced Jake.

"Who's Lulu?" Jake raised an eyebrow.

"His car." Paige smiled.

"Of course," Jake laughed, grabbing Paige's suitcase and opening the front door of the inn. Paige picked up the backpack and paused briefly on the threshold to accept a kiss from Jake before she stepped inside.

CHAPTER TWO

Appealing and romantic, those were the words that had come to mind when Paige thought about the old steam trains for *The Manhattan Post* article. But the terms took on new meaning when she considered Jake's presence on this trip. She would have to balance work and personal time carefully to make sure the visit to Hutchins Creek didn't become a romantic escape, or at least not merely one. It wouldn't be a problem. Jake always respected her work assignments.

Footsteps signaled someone approaching. Jake had set Paige's suitcase near a sturdy oak registration counter that appeared to be original to the inn, according to the similar trim around doorframes. A carved banister along stairs leading to a second floor matched the same wood.

"Paige MacKenzie, I take it, seeing as this fine gentleman accompanied you inside."

The woman who took a place behind the counter was friendly in a matter-of-fact manner. Paige estimated her to be in her early fifties. A well-worn blue work shirt with the sleeves rolled up revealed strong-looking, but bony wrists. The blue softly complemented her hair, a rich brown with a few wisps of gray. The smile on her lean face was welcoming.

"Rose Hutchins," she said, opening a hefty volume of handwritten records and turning it to face Paige. "We do things the old-fashioned way around here." She handed Paige a pen and pointed to a line in the book. "Just sign your name next to Room 24. We have you in the San Juan room. Mr. Norris is in the Prospector room, next door. An adjoining door opens to turn the two rooms into a large suite if you like. We're finishing tidying up the suite now. It will just be a short wait."

"Sounds perfect," Paige said. "And I love the names of the rooms. Those are train names, right? I did some pre-trip research and remember reading those."

"You're exactly right," Rose said. "All our rooms are named after trains that ran on the Denver-Rio Grande line. Mountaineer, Rio Grande Zephyr, Exposition Flyer, Shavano and Silver Vista are others. Each room is different. We keep the doors open when they're not occupied, so you're welcome to look inside, Ms. MacKenzie."

"Please call me Paige."

"As long as you call me Rose," she replied, smiling.

Paige returned the smile. She was warming up quickly to the innkeeper.

"Make sure you visit the railroad museum while you're here," Rose said. "Fascinating history exhibits there. You'll find a brochure in your room. You're a reporter, right? I'm sure you're already planning to stop by there. You'll certainly pick up plenty of information."

"Absolutely," Paige said. "It's one of the reasons I decided to stay in Hutchins Creek. I had hoped to stop by there this afternoon."

Rose glanced at a tall grandfather clock. "You can still make it, but you'll have to hurry. The museum closes at four o'clock and it's already past three. Let me try to catch Henry. He can run you back down there. The museum is on Main Street, right behind the train depot. It's walking distance, but it'll be faster if he gives you a ride."

With a quick dash to the front door and back, Rose returned. "I just caught him as he was pulling out. Go on down and take a look around. You probably won't have time to see all the indoor exhibits, but there are outdoor displays in back. You can always wander around there. Jesse doesn't mind people poking around after hours. The area isn't locked."

"Who is Jesse?" Paige asked.

"Jesse Hutchins, my younger brother, runs the museum."

Paige turned to Jake. "What do you think?"

Jake laughed. "I think you're eager to get digging for information, and the suite's not ready yet, anyway. I have a few business calls to make. Why don't I get those out of the way while you go check out the museum? Then we can have a nice dinner. I'm sure Rose can suggest a place."

Rose nodded her head. "A couple of great options come to mind. You two can look at menus before you go out. I especially recommend The Iron Horse."

"It sounds like a perfect plan," Paige said.

"Except for one thing. I'm not sure letting you explore on your own is a good idea," Jake continued, trying to hold back a grin. "You promise not to snoop around in places where you're not invited?"

"Absolutely," Paige said. She, too, tried to keep a straight face. Jake knew his suspicions were justified, whether she denied them or not. Fortunately, from where he was standing, he couldn't see her fingers crossed behind her back.

* * *

The Hutchins Creek Railroad Museum, at two stories, was larger than the neighboring buildings. Despite a need for a fresh coat of paint, it seemed to demand respect, as if it were stating its importance. Hutchins Creek was, after all, a town built around the railroad. Without that particular history, it wouldn't exist.

Paige took in the red paint, reminiscent of a country barn. Small, paned windows ran along the front of both the lower and upper floors of the structure. A brick walkway led up to the front steps, each brick with an individual or family name inscribed on it. A few were dedicated to the memory of lost loved ones. Others celebrated local schools or businesses. All spoke of community.

Although not part of the current railroad depot, the museum stood not far away. Because of the train tracks extending from behind the building, Paige suspected it was the original town station and that the route had been diverted onto newer tracks.

After she studied the outside of the museum, Paige climbed the steps and pulled on the door's heavy iron handle. The door was a mass of solid walnut with a rounded upper edge. It was as if the thick wood contained knowledge and secrets it didn't share with the town residents. Her curiosity piqued, Paige couldn't wait to get inside.

The museum's interior reminded Paige of the inside of a train depot: plenty of room for seats and waiting areas. A sales counter had been fashioned around a small section that served as a gift shop. Other counters and racks displayed books and novelty items. A cash register sat in the sales area, looking like a modern outcast amidst the nostalgic contents of the old building. Historical or not, modern businesses needed to embrace technology to survive the economy. Paige had used a combination of technology via the internet plus old-fashioned research methods to gather enough information to give her an inkling of Hutchins Creek's history.

Jesse Hutchins was not hard to spot. He bore a striking resemblance to Rose, though he was a good decade younger. He stood behind the counter in a light blue shirt and darker blue striped overalls. A red bandana and requisite matching striped hat topped off the traditional engineer outfit. One hand cradled a model train engine, the other, a tiny screwdriver. He appeared not to hear Paige enter despite a train whistle that sounded as she passed through the doorway. She admired his concentration and took advantage of it to look around before introducing herself.

Starting to her right, she followed a wall displaying old black and white photos of the early town. The first photograph confirmed her assumption that the museum building had once been the train station. Although the doorway to the station would have been on the opposite side of the building, there was no doubt it was the same structure. The roofline and windows were the same. The tracks Paige had seen from outside fit that theory, as well. The front and back of the building were simply reversed now, in keeping with the unused tracks and Main Street being the access point.

A second picture showed a proud group standing in front of the same building. An elderly man stood in the middle, hands in his overall pockets. A second man stood to his right with a hand on the first man's shoulder. And a tiny boy posed to the left, one foot resting on a small barrel. A gold plaque below the photo identified the three men of various ages as Jasper Hutchins, Jerome Hutchins and Jesse Hutchins. Engraved along with the three names were the words "Three generations" and the date "1968."

"Now, if Great-grandfather Jed had still been around, we could have had four generations in that photo."

Paige spun around at the sound of the deep voice to find Jesse Hutchins only a few feet away. He still held the model engine and pointed at the picture with the screwdriver as he spoke.

"He would have been one hundred six years old when that picture was taken, though. That's why he's not in it. Born in 1862 and died in 1944. Never met him, obviously. Just heard stories, like everyone else."

"He must have been a fascinating man," Paige said. "Establishing a town like this, back in those days." Paige paused, automatically ready to shake Jesse's hand, but she realized both hands were full. She settled for a verbal greeting. "I'm Paige MacKenzie, by the way."

"Oh, I know who you are, ma'am," Jesse laughed. His smile seemed to lighten his dark brown eyes and matching hair, making him look even younger. "You're the reporter from New York. Rose told me all about you coming out here to learn about the railroad."

"Yes, I'm researching an article on old steam trains, along with some history on the development of the railroad system out West."

"Then you've come to the right place," Jesse said. "There's plenty of history in Hutchins Creek. And we can teach you all about those steam trains. Did you ride in on the one from Durango?"

"I did," Paige said. "It was quite the adventure. I'd never been on a steam train before."

"You don't say. Well, you do have a few back East, you know."

"Yes, that's true, Paige said. "But yours represents the Old West and the development of the railway system out here. Plus, I've never visited this area, so that made this all the more appealing."

"It's your first time out West?" Jesse raised his eyebrows.

"Oh no," Paige said quickly. "I've been to Wyoming, Montana and New Mexico this past year to research other articles. But this is the first time I've been to Colorado."

"Well, you'll enjoy it here. The Rocky Mountains are mighty beautiful, and the railroad history is filled with all sorts of interesting facts, as well as some legends. This is a great town, too, if I do say so myself. Of course, our family founded it. But it would be great even if they hadn't. Excuse me..."

Jesse walked away to greet a new visitor, so Paige took advantage of the time to look at the other framed photographs. Some recorded town events and highlighted social gatherings involving important guests who had arrived by train, senators and celebrities among them. Others were specific to the trains themselves, detailing improvements in railway cars and equipment over the years. A few documented the construction of the new station – hardly new anymore, some fifty years later – and the addition of train tracks in front of the new building. Images of a ribbon-cutting ceremony, the christening of a new engine, and several interior shots of elegant Victorian passenger cars filled the rest of the wall.

Paige moved on to a glass display case filled with railway parts. The wide variety of spikes, switches, braces, cross ties, fastenings, beams, girders and stringers made Paige feel glad she was only there to write about the railway, not to build it. Mechanics and electronics had never been her strong suit.

Paige then came across a detailed model of an old train car. Enclosed in glass, the miniature version of an elegant railway car was as exquisite as it was precise. Each tiny window, doorway and step was intricately formed and painted. It looked like a toy, yet much too refined.

"Beautiful, isn't it?" Jesse said.

"Yes, it's remarkable." Paige turned her head sideways to get a better look inside. Tiny rows of seats filled the car, each bench-type structure in line with a window. Impossible though it would be, the urge to climb inside almost overwhelmed her.

"That's The Morning Star," Jesse said. "A fine local artist made that model. But you can see the real thing out back."

"Really?" Paige straightened up, hoping she hadn't misunderstood. "Out back?"

Jesse nodded. "We have a few of the older cars outside. The Morning Star is on the center tracks. It's not as shiny as that model, though. That car was used for a good fifty years, first on the section of the San Juan Extension that ran from Antonito to Durango, and then on the Durango-Silverton line. The museum acquired it in the 1980s, but it's been sitting out there weathering since then. We're working on raising money to restore it, but we've got a ways to go. There's a fundraiser coming up. Hopefully it'll draw in some donations."

"You said it's on tracks? Does that mean it runs?"

"No," Jesse said. "I mean, it could. There's nothing wrong with it mechanically, and the tracks still connect with the main rails. But it's a museum exhibit now. We take it down the tracks a bit now and then, when we move cars around. But I don't think it's moved more than that in a good thirty years, maybe longer. It was a beauty in its heyday, though. I rode in it when I was a youngster."

"You did?"

"Yes, indeed. It was my grandfather's favorite car. My dad's, too. He was so proud of it. Kept it spiffed up all the time. Never quite knew why he was so fond of that one in particular, but he was."

"Well, if it looked anything like this model in those days, I can understand it. I'd want to ride in it, too." Paige took one more look at the model and then turned and searched for the back door.

"Right there," Jesse said, pointing to an "exit" sign on a far wall. "I've got to start closing up the register, but feel free to look around."

"Thank you, I will. Do you have any printed information on the museum? Something with more history and photos than the brochure at the inn? I'd like to look it over tonight."

Jesse circled back to the counter and pulled a small book from a standing rack, handing it to Paige. "This will give you more background information than the brochure. You should have it, anyway, for your article." Jesse waved away Paige's attempt to pay him for the book. "Come back tomorrow and I'll be glad to show you around and answer any other questions you have."

"That sounds great," Paige said. Promising to stop by the next day, she exited through the back door.

CHAPTER THREE

The museum's back yard was neither formally arranged nor exactly haphazard. A "work in progress" would best describe it, Paige decided. Several train cars sat in different sections of the yard, each in varying states of restoration. Smaller items filled spaces between the large cars, most mechanical or technical – probably important to a functioning railroad, yet unfamiliar to Paige. An impressive collection of old signage covered the back, outside wall of the museum. Some represented Hutchins Creek, but a few named other towns along the route.

The Morning Star rested on tracks in the center of the yard, obviously the main attraction of the outdoor area. It barely resembled the miniature model inside. It not only lacked the elegance of new paint, shiny metal and polished details, but its exterior was faded and cracked, with peeling paint and numerous scratches. A chain stretched across the open steps, clearly intended to discourage visitors from stepping inside. A sign politely requesting donations for the restoration fund hung from the chain. Paige made a mental note to contribute to the fund before leaving Hutchins Creek. The more she visited historic towns, the more drawn she was to their stories. She liked the idea of being even a small part of restoring structures and landmarks to help preserve history for future visitors.

Paige fought the urge to unhook the chain and enter the car. Jesse was still inside closing up, and she knew she could pop back in to ask permission. Not that a little detail like permission tended to stop her, anyway. But she'd just arrived and had no pressing reason to look inside, other than curiosity.

Moving on to other parts of the yard, she took note of cars that had served different purposes. All had chains across the entrances, but either had windows low enough to see inside, or steps to enable visitors to look in. Some had signs explaining the particular car's function. A dining car, freight car and caboose offered variety to the yard's display. In addition, an old engine in relatively good condition sat on the same central tracks as The Morning Star, though they weren't attached to each other.

One of the outdoor exhibits impressed Paige most. A sizable portion of the yard contained a miniature railroad, complete with scenery and buildings. The structures were smaller than life-sized, but larger than mere toys. Although Paige suspected the area was intended for children to explore, it also provided adults with an opportunity to understand the inner-workings of the railroad. Brass placards explained the functions of coaling and switch stations. A hands-on display allowed visitors to pull switch levers. A detailed diagram explained the process of creating steam, illustrating the internal engine function of the firebox, boiler and pistons.

"Password, please."

Paige looked around for the source of the young, sweet voice, finding it easily. A young child leaned on a fence post at the far corner of the miniature railroad yard. Dressed in a white T-shirt, denim overalls and a striped engineer's cap that was a touch too big, it was clear the youngster felt personal pride in supervising that particular area.

"Railroad?" Paige ventured.

"Yep." The child stepped forward. "This is my favorite place of everywhere on earth."

"Well, I can see why it would be," Paige said. "It's a pretty cool area. I think I could learn a lot about trains here."

"I can teach you," the petite figure said. "I know all about trains."

"I bet you do," Paige said. "And I know very little about them, so you can be my instructor. I'll call you Professor..." Paige waited for a name to connect to the child.

"Hutchins. You can call me Professor Hutchins." A sound closely resembling a giggle escaped from the child's mouth. "Or else just call me 'Sam,' like everyone else. That's my real name."

"Ah, I see." Paige nodded. "Well, nice to meet you, Sam. My name is Paige. I'm visiting here for a few days, hoping to learn about the railroad."

Sam Hutchins, Paige mused. *The family finally broke away from the "J" tradition of naming sons.* As soon as this thought ran through Paige's mind, Jesse dispelled it when he leaned out the back door of the museum.

"Samantha, don't go bothering visitors, now, you hear me? I'm about done closing up. You need to be ready to go."

"That's my dad," Sam said, pulling off the engineer cap to allow long blonde tresses to tumble down. With a swift wave of one hand, she pushed some strands behind her shoulder.

"So I guessed," Paige said. "This must be a fun place to have your dad work, especially if you get to come to work with him."

"I don't come to work with him. I'd get bored if I stayed here all day. That's what he says, anyway. We live in that big house right there." Sam pointed to a two-story structure a few yards beyond the back fence. Paige noticed an open gate between the connecting yards. "I can walk here by myself, now that I'm five."

Paige smiled. "That must be great, getting to walk over here on your own."

"It's super great," Sam said. "I just call my dad on the phone, and then I stand in our back door. When he comes out and waves, I get to walk down."

"I can see that's a good plan. Did you make that up yourself?"

"Yep." Sam shrugged her shoulders. "Well, Lily helped me. That's who takes care of me. She helps me call him, too, because I'm not supposed to use the phone. I tried to call him myself once, but I called Mrs. Murphy by accident. She got really crabby just because I woke her up from a nap. I even said I was sorry and she *still* acted crabby."

Jesse's voice called out from the museum's back door again, telling Sam to get her things together. The young girl gathered up a backpack and sweater, and started for the museum, but stopped to say goodbye to Paige.

"Come back tomorrow and I'll show you around," Sam said. She lowered her voice to a whisper. "My secret treasure is here, but don't tell!" With that, she ran off, disappearing into the museum.

Amused at the youngster's antics, Paige surveyed the back yard once more and decided to call it a day. She passed through the building briefly to bid goodbye to Jesse and Sam. Turning down an offer for a ride, she pulled her sweater closer to guard against a late afternoon breeze and walked back to the inn.

* * *

Paige relaxed into the thick velvet cushions of the plush booth. The Iron Horse had been the perfect restaurant choice, just as Rose had suggested it would be. The popular train-themed eatery had beaten out the other options they considered after perusing the menus Rose kept for guests at the hotel.

Now, looking around at the classy yet casual décor, Paige was sure they'd dine at this place more than once during their stay in Hutchins Creek. Elegantly framed sketches of railroad scenes surrounded their comfortable booth. Whimsical touches on the linen-covered tabletop, such as miniature caboose salt and pepper shakers and lantern-shaped votive candle holders, picked up the train theme. Best of all, the lighting was subdued, perfect for a romantic evening.

"Can I get you folks something to drink?" The twenty-something server, identified as Abby by her name tag, set two cocktail napkins down and waited for an answer.

"I'm guessing white wine for both of us," Jake said, "but I know better than to make that decision on my own." He slid a hand across the table, encircling Paige's fingers with his own.

"He's a good guesser," Paige said, her hand and heart both warming at Jake's touch. "I'll have a glass of house chardonnay."

"And a smart man," Abby pointed out. Jake laughed and ordered the same thing.

Paige leaned forward and smiled at Jake as the server left to fill the drink order. "I can't believe you're here. I mean, I know you are, but it still doesn't feel real, even though it should after all that planning." She pinched herself. "I feel like I'm dreaming."

Jake let go of Paige's hand and placed his fingertips on top of her wrists, running them up her forearms gently and back down again. His gaze never left hers.

"Your eyes are still so blue..." Paige whispered. She almost laughed at her schoolgirl tone.

"And yours are still so green," Jake countered, not bothering to hide a grin as he matched her intonation perfectly.

Both pulled back to allow Abby to set wine glasses on the table. After they toasted their Colorado time together, they sipped the chilled chardonnay and studied the menu.

"Looks like my cowboy roots are going to be showing," Jake said. "That T-bone steak is mighty appealing with a baked potato and all the trimmings. Sautéed mushrooms and fresh cornbread, too? I think that'll hit the spot."

Paige almost choked on a second sip of wine. Her nerves were so fired up at seeing Jake in person, she wasn't sure she could even get through a salad, much less a full meal. Still, it had been a long day. Under her excitement, she knew rationally she was hungry, or at least in need of nourishment.

She scanned the menu, forcing herself to concentrate until she made a decision.

"I'll match you, but only as far as the mushrooms go," Paige said. "The parmesan-herb stuffed portabella mushroom gets my vote."

"A couple of Caesar salads to start?"

"Sounds perfect."

Paige and Jake set aside their menus. Within minutes their orders were on the way to the kitchen, and they began discussing the afternoon.

"How was your visit to the railroad museum?" Jake leaned back, one arm stretched across the top of the booth. Paige had to focus to answer the question, so appealing was the casual movement.

"Intriguing," she said, pulling herself together. "Both the museum *and* the Hutchins family. Seems there's quite a history in this town. Oh, and I met the sweetest little girl, Sam."

"Sam?"

"Samantha," Paige clarified. "She's Jesse Hutchins' daughter. He runs the museum. Wispy little, elfin creature. She told me to come back to see the secret treasure she keeps in the museum's back yard." Paige laughed as she picked up a fork for the newly arrived salads. "Imaginary treasure, I suspect."

"You do have a knack for finding secret treasures on your trips," Jake pointed out. "Maybe she'll save you the effort. Or at least help you avoid some of the scrapes and scratches you tend to get in the process."

"Very funny. But I'm after facts this time, not adventure." *Except for the romantic kind*, Paige added silently. "You know the railroad has a fascinating history."

"That I do know," Jake said, reaching for a fork. "I have an ancestor way back who worked for the Union Pacific, helped build the Transcontinental Railway, in fact."

"That makes sense. That ran right through Wyoming, didn't it?"

"Yes, it did. Straight across the southern section, westbound. Met up with the eastbound track in Utah, not far from Salt Lake City."

"At Promontory Point," Paige added. "I brushed up on that when I was researching. Though my article centers around the Denver & Rio Grande Railroad, which didn't come around until much later."

"And this line here?" Jake asked.

Paige smiled. She'd anticipated more of a romantic dinner than a work discussion, but she didn't mind filling Jake in on her newspaper assignments. The fact that he made an effort to be interested in her work was just one of many things to love about him.

Love. There was that word, spilled out in the open the last time they'd seen each other. Try as she might to set it aside when she was away from him, she knew she'd have to decide soon. He'd made his intentions clear by asking her to consider moving to Jackson Hole. She'd told him she'd think about it, and she hadn't lied. In fact, she'd barely been able to think about anything else. But it was a big step. No, it was a *huge* step. Leaving Manhattan, leaving a job she loved.

"Paige?"

"Yes?" Paige said, at a temporary loss for words.

"The line here, the railroad?"

"Of course," Paige said quickly, as if her mind had never wandered off. "The Durango-Silverton line. Are you really wondering how I chose Hutchins Creek as my base for writing this article?" Jake nodded. "That's easy. I wanted to get a feel for the old steam trains, the original engines used when the rail system was built out here. And..." Paige paused. "I'm growing fond of small towns. This appealed to me more than spending a few days in Denver."

"Is that so?"

Paige eyed Jake's not-so-subtle smile and knew exactly what he was thinking. If Denver was too big to enjoy for a few days, Manhattan might be headed for the history books soon.

The arrival of their main course saved Paige from commenting, and she took advantage of the interruption to change subjects.

"How are things going at your ranch?"

Jake laughed. "Come back with me and see."

Walked right into that one.

"Seriously, Jake," Paige prodded.

"Seriously? I could use more help," Jake admitted. "Might hire a couple of local guys to help fix up those old cabins. I replaced some floorboards, but then got sidetracked with fence repairs. Something always needs doing."

"It's a big property," Paige pointed out, thinking of the acreage he'd purchased when he first moved from Cody to Jackson Hole. "Seems reasonable you'd hire some workers."

"Well, summer's almost here. That's the time to get things done, when the weather cooperates."

They continued their conversation through dinner and lingered over a shared slice of blackberry cobbler and two coffees until, stomachs full and bill paid, they headed back to the inn.

CHAPTER FOUR

"Jed Hutchins was our great-grandfather. Founded this town in 1887. He was just twenty-five years old, newly married and working up in Silverton laying down tracks for a new line up to Ouray."

Rose Hutchins sat in a wing-backed chair, a cup of tea in her lap. Paige and Jake had both politely turned down her offer of tea and dessert, saying they were full from the meal they'd just finished at The Iron Horse.

"He was so young," Paige mused, "to settle down and start a town."

"Well, a person's got to lay his head somewhere," Rose said. "Might as well be your own town. Plus I think he had a vision of sorts, felt there'd be a need for a town somewhere between Durango and Silverton. Of course, there are a few now. But back then, this was about it."

"He was a railroad man his whole life?" Jake asked.

"Yes he was. All of the Hutchins men were at one time or another: Jed's son, Jasper, then Jasper's son, Jerome, and now Jesse." Rose counted the generations on her fingers as she recited the names. "Jasper and Jerome both worked some odd jobs for a while, but they came back to the railroad, just like the others."

"Gosh, Jake, you'd fit right in with this family." Paige grinned.

"That's certainly true," Rose said. "How we didn't end up with a 'Jake' in that bunch, I have no idea. Maybe we should adopt you."

"You managed to escape the tradition," Paige pointed out.

Rose laughed, almost spilling her tea. "Only if you count the name 'Jane Rosemary Hutchins' as an escape."

"I see," Paige grinned. "I should have guessed."

"Jesse doesn't have a son?" Jake said.

Rose shook her head. "No, but he has a lovely daughter. She had just turned one when her mother passed away. Jesse has been raising her and doing a fine job. She spends a lot of time with me, but they have their own place and a part-time housekeeper, Lily, who watches her when he's working."

"In a house behind the museum," Paige added.

"Yes, that's right," Rose said. "How did you know?"

"I met Sam at the museum. That is, behind the museum."

"Oh, of course," Rose said. "Samantha – officially Jessica Samantha - loves it there. She considers that miniature train yard to be her own personal territory."

"I can vouch for that," Paige laughed. "But she's a lovely ambassador for that display. She's invited me back tomorrow to see her 'special treasure.'"

"Yes, the treasure." Rose smiled, a twinkle in her eye. "Be prepared to hold it delicately. It won't be hard. It's very light."

"Weightless is my guess," Paige ventured.

"You're a perceptive young lady," Rose laughed.

"Tell me, when did the museum open? Did Jesse start it? He must have his hands full, running the business and raising a child."

"No," Rose clarified. "Jerome – who's our father, but I'll use first names to help you keep the family history straight – started the museum when the train station moved to the new building in the '80s. Jesse took it over when Jerome passed away. Jesse's done a good job keeping it going, but Jerome was the original force behind it. He was determined to get that museum going. He organized fundraisers and brought in equipment and old train cars for displays – especially The

Morning Star. We weren't allowed to touch it after he finally brought it in. His father, Jasper – our grandfather – actually worked on that very car, back when it was still running. So it had sentimental value to him – for that reason, I guess. He was obsessed with it."

"The model of it inside the museum is exquisite," Paige said.

"That's Jesse's doing," Rose said. "Since Jerome's wishes kept him from working on the actual train car, he settled for making the model, instead. Did a fine job, too."

"Looks like you have plans to restore it now. I saw the sign for donations hanging on the chain at the car's entry."

"Yes, we hope to start on that later this year. Dad was so opposed to having anyone touch it that we felt we couldn't go against his wishes," Rose said. "But it's in the best interest of the museum to restore it. Visitors love the model. You can imagine the response if they could tour the actual car."

Paige held back her thoughts, knowing it was unlikely the train car's chain would keep her out. At least she admitted her incurable curiosity, if only to herself. Besides, there was always a possibility Jesse would give her permission to see the inside of the train car, maybe to help her write authentic descriptions for her article.

"You know, Rose, it might spur some donations if I mentioned The Morning Star in my article. It would be easy to work that angle in. Restoration is part of keeping the history of the old railroad days alive." Paige wanted to pat herself on the back for thinking of this. Not only would it make interesting reading, but it was likely to gain her access to the car.

Rose's face lit up. "That would sure be nice for us. Might bring a few more visitors into the museum, too. Jesse would like that. He tries so hard to keep those exhibits going, but it takes money to run the place."

"Of course it does," Paige said. "And you're right here along the Durango-Silverton line. Plenty of tourists pass through here. Maybe we can get more to stop in."

"I like the way you think," Rose said. "I'll pass your ideas on to Jesse when I see him next."

"I'm sure Paige will be back there tomorrow," Jake said, a grin stretching across his well-tanned face. "Wouldn't be like her to get an idea in her head and not dive right in."

"Well, I find that admirable," Rose said. "Perseverance is a good trait. It's how things get done. And speaking of exactly that, I'd better get to preparing tomorrow's breakfast. You two make yourselves comfortable," Rose added as she stood up. "Think of Hutchins Creek Inn as your home away from home."

"We'll do that, ma'am." Jake stood up as Rose did. "We appreciate your hospitality."

"Yes," Paige agreed immediately. "And a lovely home it is. Thank you, Rose. And thank you also for filling us in on the family history."

"Well. There's a lot more than just the family tree," Rose laughed. "But I have a feeling by the time you leave here, you'll know even more about this Hutchins family than I do."

"I wouldn't doubt that for a minute," Jake laughed.

"Coffee and tea will be set out in the lobby by 7 a.m. Breakfast is served from 8 to 9. Good night," Rose added before disappearing into the kitchen.

Jake smiled as he took Paige's hand and gently pulled her to her feet. Clearly remaining on the couch in the inn's front parlor was not what he had in mind for the evening.

It only took a short walk down the hall to arrive at the doorways to their adjoining rooms. Paige paused outside her door, key in hand, while Jake put on a dramatic show of checking all his pockets and coming up empty.

"What do you know," he said with mock seriousness. "I seem to have forgotten my key." He leaned one arm against Paige's door, the other slipping around her waist.

"You're a terrible liar," Paige said, grinning and blushing simultaneously. "But I suppose you could enter here and use the connecting door to your room."

"Exactly my thought," Jake said.

Stepping into the room with Jake behind her, Paige barely had time to close the door and turn around before Jake slipped his hands around her face, caressing her cheekbones with his thumbs. "Do you have any idea how much I've missed you? I've been waiting all day to do this." He placed a soft kiss on her forehead, followed by others on each eyelid. Paige's pulse quickened as he trailed his lips along her cheeks and finally to her mouth, first bestowing a light, tender kiss and then letting passion take over. Paige was grateful for the sturdy door as he pressed against her. She wouldn't have trusted her legs to hold her up without the solid wooden support behind her.

"I've missed you, too," Paige whispered, her voice barely audible as she buried her face in Jake's neck. The familiar scent of his skin comforted her, as if she'd just returned from a trip away instead of being at the beginning of one. More and more she realized that home wasn't a specific place; it was wherever Jake was. Living two thousand miles apart was becoming increasingly difficult. A decision about moving west was an unspoken current in the air.

"Paige," Jake whispered. His lips caressed a spot below one ear and headed downward slowly. He slipped an edge of her T-shirt aside with one hand to kiss her shoulder, his other hand sliding around her waist.

"Shhh," Paige said, running her hands down Jake's back and giving in to the luxury of being in his arms. "No talking. Not right now." The time together was worth savoring. No conflict, no decisions, just this moment.

CHAPTER FIVE

Paige arrived the following morning to find Sam already in the Hutchins Creek Railroad Museum's back yard. Dressed in a faded, flowered gauze skirt and pink tank top, the young girl looked every bit the waif she had the day before.

"Skinny as a string bean. I'm surprised she doesn't blow away in the wind."

Jesse's voice took Paige by surprise. She'd entered through the museum's back gate, rather than the front, and hadn't yet seen Jesse.

"Good morning," Paige said. "I apologize for letting myself in the back. I saw Sam out here and wanted to say hello."

"No need to apologize. Front entrance, back entrance — doesn't matter to me how people enter, as long as they enter."

"Do you get many visitors?"

"Not as many as we used to," Jesse said. "Locals have seen all the exhibits already. Sometimes they use our back room for meetings and such. But the main visitors we get are people who stop in Hutchins Creek along the route between Durango and Silverton."

"How many is that?"

As Jesse scratched his head, his engineer hat slipped off-center. He left it askew, and Paige had a crazy urge to straighten it for him. She refrained.

"Maybe a dozen in a day. Or two dozen on a Saturday or Sunday."

"That's a shame," Paige said. "With all these exhibits and history you have here?"

"We've got a lot here, but not much is new. We're working on this back yard, hoping it'll draw more people. But there's a lot more work to be done."

"I noticed the donation sign yesterday, the one hanging on The Morning Star. Is that your main project now?"

Jesse shrugged his shoulders. "We're hoping for it to be. We would have started it a long time ago if Dad had been open to the idea. Stubborn man, that one. He let us restore other cars, but not that one."

"Any particular reason?" Paige watched Sam skipping around inside the miniature train area, a self-assigned caretaker of her tiny kingdom.

"Only that he'd always been more sentimentally attached to that one. We figure he wanted it to stay the way he remembered it."

"I'd think being attached to it would make him even more eager to see The Morning Star restored, so visitors could see what it looked like in its heyday," Paige said.

Jesse turned his head toward the museum at the sound of a train whistle, a signal that someone had entered through the front. "Yes, that would seem logical. But Jerome Hutchins was the epitome of stubborn. He insisted that car should stay as it is. Said it was good for people to see the old as well as the new. I guess he had a point." He signaled toward the whistle to excuse himself. "Visitors," he pointed out. "I need to greet them."

Paige nodded but remained behind. Sam had stopped flitting around and appeared focused on a project. Paige couldn't resist the urge to check it out, suspecting it might have to do with the "secret treasure." Imaginary or not, the idea was still intriguing. Not to mention the fact that children sometimes had information that adults didn't have. Or, better yet, more of a tendency to spill that information.

"Good morning, Sam," Paige said as she approached the wispy figure. From where Paige stood, all she could see was the gauze skirt, the back of two skinny legs and the heels of worn sneakers that might have been white at some point in the past. The rest of the girl was bent forward at the waist.

Sam straightened up at the sound of Paige's voice, waved and returned to her former position. Paige drew closer, expecting to find something fascinating enough to keep the youngster's attention. She was surprised to simply find a stack of hay.

"What are you working on?" Paige asked, growing more curious as Sam pulled one straw of hay out at a time, setting each in one of several piles.

"Just getting the hay ready. See?" Sam held up an example of two straws of equal length, setting them aside together.

"I see," Paige said. Her only other option would be to say she didn't see at all. "What do you plan to use these for?"

A giggle emerged from Sam, the type only a child can make in response to an adult's silly comment.

"I'm not going to use them, of course!" Sam laughed. "They're for the bird."

"Ah, for the bird?" Paige's comment was half-statement, half-question.

"For its nest," Sam explained, her tone serious now. "Don't you know birds need nests? They need them for homes. Like we have houses. Birds don't live in houses."

"You're right, they don't." Paige knew her best option at this point was to let the conversation proceed on its own.

"Wanna help?"

How could she turn down such a sincere request? "Sure," Paige said. "Show me what to do."

"It's easy," Sam said. She demonstrated with several different pieces of hay, holding each one up to show Paige its length – short, medium or long. "Just put them with others the same size. You can make piles on your side, and I'll make piles on my side." She set a few pieces down as examples.

"I think I understand," Paige said, finding two pieces of similar sizes and placing them together on her side of the work area.

"Very good," Sam said. "You would get a gold star, 'cept I don't have one. Those are at school. Only my teacher can give them out."

"Well, that's very nice of you to offer me a gold star, even if your teacher has them all. Too bad you don't have invisible stars," Paige added slyly. She sorted a few more strands of hay while waiting for the comment to sink in.

"Oh! I *do* have invisible stars. I forgot!" Sam ran over to an old copper pot and reached inside, returning with one fist clenched. "Here you go." She opened her hand and lifted an invisible star from her palm, pressing it against Paige's collarbone.

"Thank you!" Paige exclaimed. "I love it. It's very shiny."

Sam fixed Paige with a look that was half perplexed and half disgusted. "It's not shiny, it's *invisible!*"

Paige took the reprimand well, admitting to herself that she needed to work on her imagination etiquette.

"What are you ladies doing?"

Paige welcomed Jake's interruption since she was clearly losing ground in the current discussion.

"We're getting ready to make a bird nest," Sam explained.

"Because birds don't live in houses," Paige added, watching the amused look on Jake's face. Fortunately, he refrained from arguing that some birds *do* live in houses.

"Did you know that?" Sam asked.

Jake nodded. "I know birds don't live in the kind of houses people do."

Sam pondered his answer, her expression skeptical.

"They love nests," Jake added quickly. It seemed an acceptable qualification, as Sam went back to her task.

Paige helped sort a few more strands of hay and then stood up. "Sam, do you think you could work on your own for a bit? I'd like to show Jake the inside of the museum."

Sam nodded and kept working.

Jesse was just finishing a sale as Paige and Jake entered through the museum's back door. He placed a small replica of a steam engine in a bag and handed it to a customer who thanked him and exited through the front.

"Only the second sale so far today," Jesse said, seeing Paige approach. "Sold a few postcards earlier. But it's better than no sales at all. Gotta be grateful for every one."

"Do you have any special events coming up?" Paige wracked her brain for ways the museum could bring in some extra income. "Any programs for local schools, to learn about railroad history? I bet parents would buy souvenirs after a presentation. Or you could hold a movie night. Maybe show Butch Cassidy and the Sundance Kid."

"Why that one?" Jake asked.

Jesse laughed. "This reporter has done her research, I see. The famous cliff scene in that movie was filmed not far from here, or at least part of it was."

"What do you mean, part of it?" Jake looked confused. "Don't tell me Newman and Redford didn't do that jump. I love that scene."

"I can explain," Paige said. "They did do the jump themselves, but not into the river, which wasn't deep enough. They jumped onto a wooden platform, about six feet below the edge of the cliff. Stuntmen finished the filming back in California."

"Well, I say that still counts, then," Jake said.

"I agree," Paige said. "You wouldn't see me jumping off a cliff, even with a platform to catch me."

"Actually, I *could* see you doing that. Just another reason I worry about you when you're out on assignments." Jake laughed.

"Sounds like we have a risk-taker here." Jesse smiled, but also gave Paige a look of mock reprimand.

"Oh, I could tell you stories...." Paige grabbed Jake's arm to interrupt his sentence.

"Let me show you around the museum."

"Diversion tactic," Jake said to Jesse as Paige dragged him away from the sales counter.

Retracing her steps from the afternoon before, Paige escorted Jake around the museum, pointing out historical photos and exhibits. In particular, they spent time looking at the detail on The Morning Star model.

"Impressive," Jake said. "That must have been one gorgeous car back in the day."

Paige nodded. "It could be now, too. It's out in that back yard, waiting to be restored."

"Why waiting?" Jake leaned forward to inspect the display more closely.

"They're taking donations to restore it."

"Aren't some of the cars out back already restored?" Jake ran one hand across the back of his neck. As she did with just about every movement he made, Paige felt warmth run across her own neck and shoulders. She blushed thinking back to the night before. There was no arguing with her feelings. Being with Jake felt like being home.

"Yes, but not this one," Paige explained, gathering her wits. "Remember what Rose told us. Jerome – Jesse's father – insisted that car not be restored."

"That seems odd to me, doesn't it to you? Looking at this model, I'd think restoring the original car would be an obvious move."

Paige glanced back at the sales counter, debating bringing Jesse into the conversation, but saw he was talking with Henry, who had just arrived. Both men looked serious. She filed this impression away and turned back to Jake.

"I agree, but I guess he was sentimental about keeping it exactly as it was. Maybe he felt restoring it would take away its charm. He might have just been watching the museum budget, too. It has to be expensive to restore a train car like this."

"I'm sure you're right," Jake said. "I've seen the money that goes into restoring old automobiles. It figures a train car would cost even more, given its size."

The museum's back door opened, and Sam appeared. Paige and Jake returned to the front counter just in time to hear an animated conversation.

"Dad, we need a birdbath."

Henry waved hello to Paige and Jake, then turned to address Sam. "Just why do you need a birdbath, young lady? I don't think you'd fit in one."

"Don't be silly, Mr. Henry," Sam giggled. "It's not for me, it's for the bird." She turned to Jesse, serious again. "Please, Dad?"

Jesse cracked a smile, looked at Henry and shrugged his shoulders. "I don't know where she gets these ideas." He turned his gaze back to Sam. "Why do we need a birdbath?"

"So the bird can take a bath!" The young girl placed both hands on her hips, clearly annoyed at the obvious question.

"What bird?" Henry leaned one elbow on the counter, amused.

Sam pursed her lips, contemplating an answer. "It's a secret," she said, after a moment.

"Oh, I see." Henry said. "Well, I just might be able to whip something up that would work for you. Give me the afternoon to see what I can do."

Sam jumped up and down as if Henry had just told her it was Christmas morning. Thanking Henry, she scurried out the back door.

"That's really not necessary," Jesse said. "The child has quite an imagination. She'll be on to wanting something else soon."

"Well, she seemed pretty darn serious about that birdbath, and it's nothing I can't whip up with a post and a bowl. It'll give me something to do, keep me out of trouble."

"Then it's a good thing," Jesse said. "We can't have you working on Lulu all the time."

"I think it's nice to see a child asking for something simple," Paige said, "instead of toys or electronics. It's refreshing."

"You've got a good point there," Jesse agreed. "Everything she needs seems to be out in that back yard."

"All right, then. I'm off to see if I can come up with a plan for a birdbath." Henry said his goodbyes and headed out the front door.

"And I think we're off to find lunch somewhere," Jake said, turning to Paige. "What do you think?"

"Lunch special at the Rails Café is always good," Jesse offered. "Two doors down."

"Perfect," Paige said, looking at Jake. "Let's go."

CHAPTER SIX

The Rails Café nestled between an old bookstore and a small market with a sign announcing a sale on peaches. Although not as elegant as The Iron Horse, it scored just as high on the railroad nostalgia scale. The quaint eatery offered cozy booths with locomotive-themed placemats and napkins, a menu featuring cleverly named options and a working model railway that circled the interior of the café. Paige found it charming. Jake showed more interest in the food than the décor.

"I think I'm going for the Boxcar Burger," Jake said. "And a Mainline Milkshake. How about you?"

"What?" Paige looked at Jake as if he'd spoken a foreign language.

"Lunch. What looks good to you?"

"I haven't even looked," Paige said, twisting in her seat in order to take in the surroundings. "Look at all this railroad memorabilia. It's fascinating. Almost like a second museum, though not as historically based." She picked up the menu, but didn't open it. "I love the old wooden railroad crossing sign by the front door. And the lyrics to *I've Been Working on the Railroad* painted along the wall below the model train tracks."

"Personally, I'm fond of that sign over the kitchen pass-through," Jake said. "The one that says 'Full Steam Ahead.' Because it implies we'll be eating soon."

"OK, I can take a hint," Paige laughed and browsed the food choices. "I'm not even sure what some of these are.

Look at this one." She pointed to a line on the menu. "Tie Hack Tamale? I don't even know what that is."

"Oh, that's easy," Jake said. "It's sort of like a burrito, but wrapped in a corn husk…"

"Stop it," Paige laughed. "You know what I meant."

"Ah, I understand now," Jake continued, grinning. "Just giving you a hard time. Tie hacks were workers who logged lumber to make railroad ties. A lot of that was done in Wyoming. We even have a memorial in the Wind River region. But northern Colorado had some activity, too."

"Well, I'll take the Short Line Salad with the Cajun Caboose Croutons," Paige finally decided. "And a glass of Iced Trestle Tea."

"Good choices." A spunky server dressed in an engineer outfit arrived in time to hear Paige's selection. Jake added his order, and the server hurried away.

"See? Full steam ahead. I like this place," Jake said.

Paige nodded in agreement as the model train above started rolling along the tracks. A young boy at a nearby table pointed to it and squealed with glee; his mother hushed him.

"Thomas!" the child cried out, clapping his hands.

Jake looked at Paige, puzzled. "Thomas?"

"Thomas the Tank Engine," Paige explained.

"Is that 'The Little Engine That Could?'" Jake asked.

"No," Paige laughed. "We'll need to educate you on your train literature."

"I've read *Murder on the Orient Express*. Does that count?"

"Absolutely," Paige said. "That's a classic, a great one, at that."

The server returned to place one milkshake and one iced tea on the table.

"What angle do you plan to take for your article this time?" Jake asked. "General railroad history? Information specific to the Durango-Silverton line?"

"I'm not sure yet," Paige admitted, sipping her tea. "It depends on how much I can learn in Hutchins Creek. I may find enough background to make a small town story feasible.

How this particular railroad town came to be, for example. That might work, since a railroad man founded it. Otherwise, I'll need to expand it to incorporate a broader scale. Perhaps the Denver-Rio Grande Line itself. I'll email Susan with some ideas later to see what she thinks."

"Your editor usually agrees with your pitches," Jake said. "I'm sure you'll come up with something this time that works for her."

"I'd like to come up with something local. Seems like four generations of railroad work, plus the founding of this town, would make a good story."

The server approached the table and delivered the rest of the meal. Paige stole a fry from Jake's plate immediately. Playfully, he pretended to brush her hand away.

"You certainly have some interesting characters here. You do always seem to find them in these small towns." Jake took a bite of his Boxcar Burger, preventing him from continuing that thought. Paige picked it up immediately.

"Quite a few people here have been around for a long time, which is a huge plus. The local residents might have information that isn't in the history books."

"Right. Obviously the Hutchins family, seeing as how they founded the town." Jake took a second bite.

"Yes, but also consider Henry. He knows this town well. He could provide a perspective from outside the Hutchins family. More objective, I think. You have to figure family might be protective about a town their ancestor founded. Henry could throw some color into the mix." Paige popped a crouton into her mouth, nodding with approval at the Cajun flavoring.

"What do you make of the girl at the museum?"

"Sam?" Paige asked. "Intriguing. Unusual. Imaginative."

"Has she shown you that 'secret treasure' yet?" Jake's smirk told Paige he wasn't asking a serious question, yet she was prepared with a serious answer.

"Not yet, but don't be so sure there isn't anything. She has a vivid imagination, but she might also have a real item that's a treasure to her, though it might not be to us. Maybe a stone she found. Or a bird feather – that would tie in with the small nest she's making."

"Good thought," Jake said, impressed. "I would never have thought of that. I bet you're great with children."

Paige was silent as she absorbed the statement. They'd never talked about children. Although they'd been on the brink of committing to future plans, those plans weren't yet defined. Jake's suggestion that she move to Jackson Hole was a constant unspoken undercurrent in their relationship.

"I love children," Paige said, and as she spoke realized how true this was. She had friends in New York with children, and she always delighted in spending time with them, whether she accompanied them on outings or just relaxed at their homes. She found reading to children especially rewarding. An avid reader herself, she loved watching children discover new worlds through books.

Paige ventured a quick look up from her salad, finding a smile on Jake's face. She felt this wasn't time for a serious discussion, so she looked back down and changed the subject. "I wonder how far along the museum's fundraising campaign is for The Morning Star's restoration. I might go back after lunch to find out."

"Really?"

"Yes, really," Paige repeated. "Restoration of old train cars could be an interesting angle for the article, if I tie it in with railroad history. Besides, I'm curious."

"About the donation status?" Jake sounded and looked confused.

"Not just that," Paige admitted. "I'm wondering if Sam might be willing to share what her secret treasure is. And…this will sound odd, but I had the strange feeling Jesse and Henry were discussing something tense when Henry first arrived."

"Based on what?"

"On their expressions, mostly. I couldn't hear what they were talking about before we walked over. I just felt...it's hard to explain. My instincts tell me something was up."

"Uh oh," Jake said. He pushed his empty plate to the side. "When your instincts get involved, you always end up in trouble."

"That's not fair," Paige protested. "Sometimes my instincts lead me to information I wouldn't have otherwise. I can't help it. It's the reporter in me."

"And other times, you end up hopping fences or trapped in tunnels."

"Not all the time." Paige's voice weakened, knowing it was hardly a defense.

"Eighty percent of the time."

"Forty percent."

"Sixty..."

"Fifty...and that's my final offer." Paige smiled. How could he argue with that? She was admitting outright that half the time she followed her hunches, she ended up in some sort of trouble.

"All right, I'll go along with fifty, but please don't go crashing through any museum floors, you hear?"

Paige barely suppressed a laugh. Jake's serious tone made her want to hug him, an urge she was having more and more frequently.

"The museum probably doesn't even have a basement," she argued. Even as she said it, a parallel thought struck her. Maybe it did? If so, could there be additional displays stored there?

Paige pushed her salad plate to the edge of the table just as the server came by.

"Can I interest you in a slice of Pullman Pecan Pie?"

Jake laughed and looked at Paige. "How do you find these towns where we can gain ten pounds in just a few days?"

Paige and the server exchanged looks and rolled their eyes. Jake's slim, muscular body wasn't likely to gain a single pound, no matter how much he ate. Paige, on the other hand, would be out for a morning run every day to keep her own slender figure. Declining dessert, they asked for the check.

"Business calls to make, for your ranch?" Paige asked as they exited the café.

"Trying to ditch me?"

"Is it that obvious?" Paige laughed. "Seriously, come back to the museum with me if you want to."

Jake shook his head. "No, I think I'll let you get in trouble all on your own. I need to contact the lumber company about a new shipment I need for the cabins."

"Good...I mean, that sounds perfect," Paige said. "I'll see you at the inn later."

"Be careful." Jake placed a soft kiss on Paige's forehead and left.

CHAPTER SEVEN

As Paige approached the museum's entrance, she heard a faint murmur of voices. She would have gone on in had she not heard the words "missing money" as she reached for the door handle. Noting a window slightly open to one side, she stepped closer to listen, leaning against the wall and checking her cell phone as a cover for her eavesdropping.

"It wasn't that much at first. Just a few dollars here or there, I figured."

Paige easily recognized the voice as Jesse's. He sounded more baffled than angry.

"That could have been anyone. You're not always up here in front. Maybe it's a teen, out to cause trouble, not after the money itself." Henry's voice. The conversation paused.

Paige held still, hoping they hadn't noticed her presence. Still, eyes focused on her cell phone, she had an excuse ready.

"I don't understand," Jesse continued. "It seems every time we get ahead, a little more disappears."

The sound of a cash drawer opening and closing followed.

"You could put in a security camera," Henry suggested.

"That's mighty expensive. We're not talking large amounts here, usually just a ten, or sometimes a twenty. It's not like someone's cleaning out the register. I'd rather take the money for a security camera and put that into the restoration fund. We don't need some fancy electronic surveillance system."

"Just tryin' to help," Henry said. "Anyway, I'm off to finish the birdbath for that daughter of yours."

"She'll appreciate that."

"I know she will, sweet thing. You're doing a good job raising her, Jesse. I'll try to bring something by for her later today. If not, I'm sure I can manage tomorrow."

Even though Paige knew Henry was about to emerge from the museum, the speed of his exit startled her. Her supposed focus on the cell phone, along with nips of guilt about eavesdropping, made her surprise at seeing him seem genuine.

She stifled her jumpiness.

"Henry, hi there."

"Paige, good to see you again. I thought you and that Jake fellow went off to lunch."

"We did," Paige said, sliding her phone into her jeans pocket. "Just finished. That's a great lunch place, The Rails Café."

"Yes, indeed. They've got the best pecan pie this side of the Mississippi. Did you try it?"

Paige laughed and relaxed. "Not today, but it was tempting. Maybe tomorrow."

"What brings you back by here so soon?"

"I wanted to check on…" Paige paused. Mentioning the donation fund seemed unwise after the conversation she'd just overheard. "…the timeline for the Durango-Silverton line. When it was built, how often it ran, that type of thing. For the article I'm working on."

Henry pulled a bandana out of his pocket and ran it across his forehead. "Well, you can get all that information inside, but I can tell you the basics. The line started running back in 1882, after the company spent about a year putting down tracks from Durango to Silverton. Used it to haul gold and silver out of the San Juan Mountains."

"No passengers?"

"Sure, there were passengers from the start. The railroad knew they could promote it as a scenic route. But it was critical for transporting ore from the mines. Served both purposes."

"And then Hutchins Creek came along in 1887," Paige said.

"Yes it did. That's when they put in a new line from Silverton to Ouray. Jed Hutchins worked on that line. Needed a place to settle down. And a fine place he picked, too."

Henry paused to look around them, and Paige did, too. The mountain air was clean and crisp, the sky a cobalt blue. "You go on in. Jesse knows every bit of history there is. I've got to finish making that birdbath."

"That's right," Paige laughed. "I think you do."

"I've got a good start. Can't disappoint the young lady," Henry said.

"No, I can understand that," Paige said. "She seemed quite determined to get that birdbath. You must have a lot of birds up here in the mountains. Sweet of her to want to look out for them."

"We have birds here, all right. Finches, swallows and wrens. Hawks, eagles and owls. If it has feathers, you can find it here."

Paige laughed. "I'll let you get on with your task, then. Thanks for the quick facts on the railroad line. And all the fine-feathered friends, too."

With a quick goodbye, Henry walked to the street, fired up Lulu and headed off. Paige waved as he drove away, and then turned back toward the museum. Entering, she found Jesse behind the counter, pad and pencil in front of him, scribbling notes or numbers or both. She couldn't quite tell without appearing too nosy.

"Back again, I see." Jesse greeted her with a smile that bore no evidence of the troubling conversation she'd overheard from outside. "How was The Rails Café?"

"Excellent," Paige said. "You didn't steer us wrong. I loved the Cajun Caboose Croutons on my salad and that Iced Trestle Tea was excellent."

"Yep, pretty darn refreshing. And those croutons are addicting. I put them in soup, on salads, and just about anything else I can. Even eat them as snacks sometimes." Jesse shuffled some paperwork and dropped it below the sales counter. "You just missed Henry."

"No, I saw him on my way in, talked for a couple of minutes. He's off to finish the birdbath for Sam." Paige crossed the room and peered outside. The back yard was empty.

"She went home," Jesse said, watching Paige. "But she'll turn up here if Henry comes back today."

"I'll bet," Paige said. "She seems determined to care for the bird. Speaking of which, is this any particular bird she's talking about?"

"Not that I know of," Jesse said. He broke into a grin. "That girl's imagination is spectacular. I wouldn't be surprised if she's just making up stories. But we do have birds all over the place here, all sorts of varieties."

"That's what Henry said." Paige paused before changing the subject, deciding on the best approach. "I'm thinking about working the restoration angle into the article I'm writing. It seems like a good match – the history of the railroad combined with efforts to keep that history recorded for the future."

Jesse sighed, but gave no other sign that anything was wrong. "Well, I agree with you, of course. I've tried to do as much as possible to update exhibits. Not just for visitors, but for people who've lived here all their lives. Because this community was built around the railroad, that history is a part of each of our lives. It's important we preserve it."

"You're doing a great job," Paige said, looking around. "I think the museum is fascinating. I'm especially fond of that model of The Morning Star. Such wonderful detail."

"Yes," Jesse agreed. "Now if only we can get the actual car restored."

"How's that going?" A trickle of guilt ran through Paige, knowing she was trying to dig out information about something she already knew.

"Not as quickly as I'd like. We're getting donations in, but…" He paused, as if debating what to say. "But not as much as we need."

"It takes time," Paige said, for lack of another comment.

"Shouldn't be taking this much time," Jesse said. He didn't elaborate.

The train whistle sounded, and a man and a young boy entered. Jesse nodded hello to the duo. The adult headed for the historical photos along the wall, while the boy who was about five, made a beeline for the model.

"Regulars, the Porters," Jesse said, which explained why the child knew right where he wanted to go. "They come up from Durango pretty often. Used to come with the mother, too, but they got divorced a ways back. I think the dad wants to keep some things regular. They're probably staying at the inn for the night. Usually do. Nice family, even with the break up. Rose always enjoys it when they stay. Stephen has heart. I sympathize with his status as a single father."

"Makes sense to me that they visit often," Paige said. "I'd do the same if I lived close by." She kept her eyes on the boy, enjoying his fascination with the miniature train car.

Jesse excused himself to greet the Porters. Paige waved goodbye and left through the back.

Scanning the empty yard, Paige started for the side exit gate. She turned back when she heard a scuffling noise. Standing still, she listened carefully, but now, there was only quiet. Had she imagined it? No, it had been faint, but definite.

"Sam?" No answer.

Walking the perimeter of the yard, she searched for the source, but found nothing and no one. Except for a light breeze, the yard was still and empty. Deciding the wind must have caused the sound, she headed back to the inn.

CHAPTER EIGHT

Paige found Jake sitting on the front porch of the inn, a laptop in front of him. A glass of lemonade sat on a nearby table, a plate of fresh-baked cookies alongside it.

"Looks like Rose is spoiling you," Paige laughed.

"That she is," Jake said, setting the laptop on the table. "And I don't mind it one bit." He caught Paige by the arm and swung her down into his lap. Wrapping his arms around her, he gently cupped one hand behind her head and pulled her close for a kiss.

"I could get used to this," Paige sighed, nestling against his shoulder.

"Exactly my plan," Jake whispered.

"I might even make you lemonade and cookies."

"Even more reason to keep you around," Jake teased.

The front door opened, and Rose set down a second frosty glass of lemonade

"Saw you coming up the walk," Rose said. "This man has been working hard out here since he returned. Maybe he'll take a break now."

"Maybe," Paige laughed. "Maybe not." She thanked Rose for the lemonade and watched her walk back inside, then turned back to Jake. "So how's the ranch work coming along?"

"Slow but steady. I'm just anxious to get as much done as possible," Jake said. He dropped his head back against the chair and rubbed Paige's shoulder with one hand.

"This is the prime season for outdoor work now, isn't it?" Paige asked, already knowing the answer.

"Absolutely," Jake said. "Once winter hits, most construction comes to a standstill. And we never know when winter might start in Wyoming."

"November? December?"

"Maybe," Jake laughed. "But it could be October, for all I know. It can snow any day of the year in Jackson Hole."

"Seriously?"

"Yes, seriously. But it's a fluke when it happens in summer, and it doesn't stick. I have several good months left to get the work done. Provided I get the supplies in and hire some help."

"Did you reach your lumber person?"

"Yes," Jake said, his tone relieved. "It should just be a few more days before the shipment comes in."

"Oh no!" Paige said suddenly. "You won't have to go back right away, will you? Not after you drove all the way down here?"

Jake laughed and kissed Paige again. "Don't you worry your pretty self about that. You're stuck with me for the week."

"Just as I hoped," Paige said. She ran one finger along the ridge of Jake's nose and laughed, then straightened up as footsteps approached. Standing, she said hello to a familiar duo walking up to the inn, suitcases in hand. Jake stood to greet them, as well.

"I believe you're the Porters," Paige said. "I saw you at the train museum. Jesse said you'd probably be staying here. I'm Paige and this is Jake."

"Glad to meet you," the man said. "I'm Stephen, and this is my son, Tommy."

"Like the train engine," Jake said, bending down to shake the boy's hand.

"That's right!" Tommy said, excited enough to drop his backpack on the porch.

Paige stifled a laugh at Jake's sudden knowledge of children's books, but she was delighted he could appear so enlightened to the child.

"A coincidence," Stephen said. "But he does love trains."

"Yes, I noticed he ran straight for the model at the museum," Paige said.

"He loves that model," Stephen said. "Every time we visit Hutchins Creek, we go by the museum. We keep hoping The Morning Star will be restored."

"You and a lot of other people," Rose said, stepping out onto the porch. She reached for one of the suitcases, but Stephen held up his hand to turn down the help.

"Rose, you always say we're like family here, so you need to let us do our part," Stephen protested. He nudged Tommy toward the front door, encouraging him to pick up the backpack.

Jake stepped forward and picked up one of the suitcases Stephen had set down. He disappeared into the inn with the new arrivals following him. He returned after a minute and sat down.

Paige pulled up a second chair. As tempted as she was to settle back on Jake's lap, she realized they were on the inn's front porch in plain sight of the world.

"It seems like that train car is a popular attraction here," Jake said. "They should get going with the restoration."

Paige took a sip of lemonade and gathered her thoughts.

"I agree," she said. "But I'm beginning to think it's more complicated than that."

"In what way?"

Paige hesitated, still forming her thoughts. "I overheard a conversation when I went back to the museum."

"You overheard a conversation?" Jake shook his head, half amused, half concerned. "Exactly where were you when you *overheard* this conversation. *Accidentally*, I suppose."

"Outside the museum."

Jake rubbed his chin. "As in, maybe, standing by an open window where you couldn't be seen? Hmm?"

"Something like that," Paige admitted. "But that's beside the point. I think…" She paused and looked around to make sure they were alone. "I think there's more delaying the restoration than lack of donations."

"What do you mean? Everyone seems to be enthusiastic about it, at least everyone we've met so far."

"That's how it seems on the surface. But I overheard…"

"…*accidentally*…" Jake prompted.

"Yes, I *accidentally* overheard…" Again Paige lowered her voice, this time to barely a whisper. "Money has been disappearing from the register."

"What? Are you sure?"

"I'm sure what I heard. Jesse and Henry were talking about it. At least, Jesse was telling Henry about it."

"How much money are we talking about?" Jake picked up his lemonade, took a drink, and set it back down.

"Not much," Paige said. "A ten or a twenty here and there. Whoever is doing this isn't clearing out the register."

"It's still theft. Not enough to hold up the restoration, though, I wouldn't think."

"True and true. Maybe just slow it down. But I don't think that's the point."

"Then what *is* the point?"

"The point is…someone doesn't want the car to be restored."

CHAPTER NINE

Paige curled up in the front room of the inn, laptop in front of her, typing in notes about railroad history. Between the information at the museum and online searches, the story was beginning to take shape. She had so many possible angles: the importance of the railroad to western commerce, the survival of area mining, the development of towns as workers settled down. She just needed to choose a direction now. That, and she needed to keep her focus, which was becoming a challenge. Even as she typed up her outline, her mind kept wandering back to the restoration efforts for The Morning Star.

Across the room, Jake sat buried in a book, a mug of coffee in one hand. They'd returned from The Iron Horse an hour before, both delighted with their second meal at the restaurant.

"Another Longmire book?" Paige didn't need to see the cover to know the answer. Jake had been binge-reading the popular Craig Johnson series for months.

"How did you guess?" Jake raised the mug of coffee to his lips, took a drink and lowered it again, his eyes never leaving the pages.

Paige smiled and looked back at her notes. She wrote; he read. No words were necessary for them to enjoy each other's company. Just sitting with him filled her with happiness.

"I know she can be a handful." Rose's voice drifted out from the kitchen. Pauses let Paige know the innkeeper was on the phone. "True, Jesse, but she's always been a bit of a tomboy. Hang in there. You'll get through these years, and the next decade, too." Paige could hear Rose chuckle as she ended the call, and for good reason. Jesse's child-rearing days were far from over.

Rose was still laughing when she walked into the front room. Paige looked up from her work and smiled. Jake raised his eyes from the book long enough to nod hello.

"Oh, don't let me bother you two," Rose said. "My brother just amuses me at times. He does a great job raising Samantha, but sometimes things throw him for a loop. Like today, when Samantha came home covered in dirt."

"Covered in dirt?" Paige smiled. She'd been the same way as a young girl, always climbing trees, never worried about being prim and proper. "That was me, as a child," Paige laughed.

"Why does that not surprise me at all?" A smile spread across Jake's face as he spoke, though his eyes stayed focused on the book.

"Well, it's not so much the dirt that's bothersome," Rose continued. "It's easy enough to throw her in the shower. But she does push the limits, crawling around in that back yard. She's been told not to, but the child's off in her own world a lot of the time. We have trouble keeping her out from under that train car, for one thing."

"Under The Morning Star?" Paige leaned forward, interested.

"Yes. It's not that it's dangerous," Rose explained. "That train is anchored well enough to stay put during an earthquake and tornado combined. We just wish Samantha would hang out in the real world now and then."

"That's understandable," Paige said, but Rose's statement distracted her. She thought back to the shuffling sound she'd heard in the museum yard and realized she'd looked *around*, but not *under* anything. It was starting to add up now. If Sam knew she wasn't supposed to be under the train car, she would have remained hidden when she heard Paige call her name.

After offering refills on coffee, Rose retreated to the back of the inn, leaving Paige and Jake alone. Jake continued reading, but Paige's thoughts had drifted away from work. Between Jesse's statements about missing donation money and Rose's comments about Sam and The Morning Star, she couldn't concentrate. She set her laptop aside, stood and stretched.

"I've been sitting too long," Paige said evasively. "I think I need to move around. Maybe I'll go for a run." She closed down the laptop and tucked it under her arm.

Jake looked up, eyebrows raised. "Don't you usually run in the morning?"

"Usually. But all these railroad details are muddled up in my mind. Running always clears my head." It was a stretch for an excuse, but Jake seemed to buy it. "And it's still light out," she added as she headed to change into running clothes.

Ten minutes later, dressed in black leggings, a violet NYU sweatshirt from college days, and running shoes, Paige jogged along the main road. Surrounded by mountain pine trees, she let the fresh air fill her lungs. Block after block, her jumbled thoughts became clearer — so clear that she was not surprised to find herself in front of the museum.

Of course, the building was closed for the night. According to the posted hours on the front door, it would reopen at ten o'clock the following morning. Paige planned to return the next day, but she was there now. *Why not look around a bit?*

Paige circled the museum, arriving quickly at the side gate to the back yard. Hadn't Rose said Jesse didn't mind people looking around the back after hours? Trying the gate, she found it unlocked. Another sign she was meant to check out the yard. Without hesitating, she stepped into the yard and closed the gate behind her.

Twilight had started falling during her run, leaving the train yard in an eerie state of semi-darkness. Emerging moonlight illuminated the ground, making it easy to walk without tripping. Yet the objects in the yard resembled silhouettes from a lateral view. She was surprised that a motion detecting light didn't spring on as she passed the building's back door. She supposed the town was small enough for the population to be trusting. Or maybe it just wasn't dark enough to trigger a light. She checked her sweatshirt pocket, grateful to find her keys. The small flashlight she kept on her keychain could come in handy if she lingered.

Paige made her way to the center of the yard where The Morning Star formed a large, dusky shape. She didn't know what she was looking for, but she circled the car as if it could tell her its story. Kneeling down, she pulled out her flashlight and directed the light under the car. The rails were still warm from the recent sunlight. Nothing appeared unusual. The space between the tracks and the car provided plenty of room for a child to play. Paige would have found it a perfect hideaway when she was a girl.

She stood and circled the car again. Her keychain-sized flashlight only illuminated an area of the welded train panels and stair railings. She'd have to wait for daylight to search inside the car. She was still convinced Jesse would give her permission to enter the car for the sake of her article. Maybe he would even allow Sam to give her a tour. She smiled at her hunch that the young girl might be more familiar with the car's interior than anyone else.

Surrounded almost entirely by darkness now, Paige was grateful for the moonlight, which sent beams of light that reflected off metal objects. Like tiny garden lights, they provided a pathway through the yard as she moved between displays. With additional help from her flashlight, she arrived at the miniature yard, Sam's favorite play area. She shared Sam's delight in this portion of the yard. Miniatures had always intrigued and enchanted her.

Paige pulled her cell phone out of her pocket, checking the time. It was getting late. After another quick trip around the smaller area, she'd head back to the inn. As it was, Jake was sure to shoot her a disapproving look when she returned.

Rose might do the same. Still, one more minute of browsing wouldn't make a difference.

Although she wasn't looking for anything specific, Paige was delighted to see a new item in the yard. Henry had followed through on his promise of a birdbath. A pole resembling a broom handle held a flat wooden board approximately five inches square. A semi-round object Paige suspected originally served as a cereal bowl rested on the flat surface. She was strongly tempted to grasp the bowl to see how Henry had attached it, but she resisted. The water inside almost reached the brim. If she spilled it, she didn't know where a spigot for water might be. If Sam had filled it herself, she could be upset to find it empty in the morning.

As Paige stepped away from the makeshift birdbath and made a quick sweep of the rest of the yard, her toe caught on a raised railing, and she tripped. She caught herself, but a second stumble sent her tumbling to the ground, hitting the birdbath on the way down. She sat up, shook her arms and legs, determined she wasn't injured, and then gathered the assorted pieces that formed the birdbath. Although the pole and board were fine, still attached to each other, the bowl was now empty. With no way to refill it, she'd need to leave it until morning.

Paige stood up and inserted the pole in the ground. Though wobbly, it stayed upright. Henry would be able to dig into the ground to secure it later. She looked around at the ground again, using her flashlight to locate the bowl. At least she could balance it on the board until the whole contraption could be firmed up in the morning. But, as she reached for the bowl, a sparkle in the moonlight caught her eye. Swinging her flashlight around, she gasped at an unexpected sight on the muddy ground. She set the bowl precariously on the board and bent down to take a closer look. Quickly determining the object merited her interest, and vowing to return it to the museum in the morning, she pocketed it and hurried back to the inn.

CHAPTER TEN

Stephen Porter flipped the coin back and forth between his fingers, his other hand holding a forkful of herbed egg frittata, one of many breakfast dishes Rose had set out for the guests. Paige, Jake and both Porters sat around a circular table, eating breakfast and discussing Paige's find.

"It's a gold coin, Paige," Stephen said. "That's the best I can tell you, other than the fact it's in mighty good shape."

"Pirate ships have gold coins," Tommy announced. "Were you on a pirate ship?"

"Not recently," Paige admitted. She tousled the boy's hair and turned to his father. "It was hard to tell what shape it was in before we cleaned off the mud."

"Nineteen twenty-six, right?" Jake asked Stephen, who still held the coin. "I think that's what we determined when Paige *finally* got back from her run last night."

Paige caught Jake's reference to her longer-than-expected excursion, but chose to ignore it. The coin was a much more fascinating topic.

"Look at the back," Paige pointed out. "See the eagle?"

Stephen handed the coin to Paige, who held it out for everyone to see.

"That's called a Double Eagle," Jake said. "It's a twenty dollar coin."

Paige looked at the coin again. "I only see one eagle."

"Double Eagle refers to the value," Jake said.

"I thought you said you didn't know much about coins," Paige said.

"I don't. But my grandfather had one like that. Kept it in his safe. He showed it to me once. It certainly didn't look as shiny as this one."

"It definitely has me curious," Paige admitted as she helped herself to a slice of cantaloupe. "I can't help wondering what it was doing in the railroad yard."

"Just like I can't help wondering what it's doing here at the inn." Jake grinned, meaning only to tease Paige. She'd made it clear she intended only to clean the coin up and take it to Jesse.

"I bet it's worth a lot of money," Tommy said. He beamed with joy at contributing to the conversation. "Especially if it came from a pirate ship."

"You never know," Paige said, smiling at him.

Rose entered the room with a fresh pot of coffee for refills. "What's all this I'm hearing about coins?"

Paige set the coin down on the table so Rose could examine it.

"Well, that's quite a pretty piece. Gold, isn't it?"

"Yes, gold," Paige said. "I found it outside the museum last...yesterday, after it closed." Jake tried to muffle his laughter, and she shot him a frustrated look. So she'd reworded her statement a bit mid-stream. Last night was, after all, yesterday. And the museum was closed when she went on her run. "I found it in the mud, outside, and brought it here to clean it up. I'm going to take it to Jesse this morning. Maybe he'll know where it came from. It might belong to someone in your family, Rose."

"Maybe," Rose mused. "But I've never seen it before. Anyone visiting the museum could have dropped it."

"Or a pirate," Tommy piped up. He waved his fork as if he were a swashbuckler with a sword. His father reached for his arm to settle him down before eggs could go flying.

"Or...a pirate..." Rose repeated, glancing around the table with amusement. "Something tells me I've missed some interesting parts of this conversation." She poured coffee for

Stephen Porter and Jake, but Paige covered her mug with her hand.

"No more coffee for me. I'm eager to get to the museum to show the coin to Jesse, see if he recognizes it."

Rose shook her head. "I'm sure he would have said something to me, especially since the museum has been struggling. If he knew about the coin, and it's valuable, he probably would have wanted to sell it to pay for The Morning Star's restoration. I doubt he's ever seen it."

"Well, only one way to find out," Paige said.

"There's a coin appraiser up in Silverton," Rose added. "If Jesse wants to check it out, I can give him the name. The guy appraised some coins for a guest recently."

"Good idea," Paige said. "I'll suggest it to him." She folded her napkin and set it beside her breakfast plate, standing up. "I think I'll head to the museum." She turned to Jake. "Coming along?"

"Not a bad idea," Jake agreed, taking a last gulp of coffee. "Who knows what you'll find next if you head down there on your own."

"I'll look up the name and number of that appraiser in case you want to get the coin checked out," Rose said.

"Thanks," Paige said. "We'll see what Jesse says."

* * *

Paige was surprised to see a crowd outside the museum; only one person stood over 48 inches high. At least twenty grade school children squirmed as their patient teacher tried to get the class to line up.

The "open" sign showed on the museum's front door, and Paige motioned for Jake to follow her inside. As she bypassed the line of schoolchildren, one young voice piped up. It belonged to the wiggliest of the bunch.

"Hey, Ms. Crandall, why do those people get to go in before us? We were here first."

The teacher smiled and waved Paige and Jake by, and then turned back to the class. "You see how nice and quiet these two people are? They are ready to visit the museum. Let me see who else is ready to go in."

As Paige opened the door, she could already hear the students calming down.

"I have a sudden urge to pull your ponytail," Jake whispered from behind her.

"Don't you dare! You'll set a bad example," Paige exclaimed. She looked over her shoulder at Jake in mock disapproval before whipping her head back to the front, causing her hair to lightly smack his face.

"Oldest trick in the book," Jake laughed. "I should've known you'd do that."

"It worked well for me when I was seven."

"And I bet you never got caught, either."

"Nope." Paige turned her head again, grinning. Jake stepped back to avoid a repeat performance.

"Good morning, you two," Jesse called from the counter. "You barely made it in while it's still safe. A wild group of second graders is about to descend on the premises. No telling what kind of commotion might break out."

"Yes, we saw them outside, lining up. They look tame enough," Paige laughed. "I think you'll survive."

"We always do." Jesse straightened a tall stack of museum brochures, enough for each child to take home after the visit. "I like having classes visit. Field trips make school more interesting, plus it's good for them to learn about the railroad since it's the foundation of our local history."

Paige made sure they were the only ones in the museum – at least at the moment – before she slid her hand into her jeans pocket and pulled out the gold coin. "Speaking of history, I was wondering if this looked familiar to you."

Jesse set the brochures aside, took the coin from Paige and inspected it, his expression blank. Paige couldn't help wondering if his lack of response was natural or intentional.

"Nice coin," he said, his tone noncommittal. "Where did you find this?"

Paige hesitated briefly before answering. "I stopped by while I was jogging last night and ended up looking around the yard. Rose had said you don't mind if people visit the outdoor exhibits after hours, and I found the coin on the ground in a muddy area. I took it back to the inn to clean it up and figured I'd bring it down to you this morning."

"A muddy area?" Jesse looked puzzled. "Hasn't been any rain lately."

"Oh, that." Paige blushed, knowing Jake was watching her explain. It wasn't the first time her clumsiness had caused problems. "I accidentally knocked Sam's birdbath over. I'll need to apologize to Henry. It didn't break, but it's unstable now, and he'll need to reattach the bowl to the board."

A burst of activity interrupted Paige's apology as the class of school children entered the museum. Although the line was orderly, the kids buzzed with enthusiasm.

"Come on in, Ms. Crandall," Jesse said. "I have a film set up in the back meeting room, ready to go. You know how to start it. After the film, I'll give everyone a tour."

As the class settled in the meeting room, the museum grew quiet again until the back door flew open, and new energy burst in.

"Dad!"

A frenzied Sam raced across the floor, ignoring Jesse's admonitions to close the door behind her.

"My bird! My bird is gone!" The anguish on Sam's face broke Paige's heart.

"Samantha," Jesse said calmly, "birds fly away. I'm sorry if you had a bird friend who's not here today."

Sam shook her head violently. "No, not this bird. This bird can't fly. But it's gone. I went to see if it had finished its bath, and it wasn't there. The water's gone, too!" She burst into tears and put her head down on the counter.

Paige looked between Jake and Jesse as the pieces fell together. She rubbed Sam's back to calm her and reached out toward Jesse with her free hand. Grasping the coin, she coaxed Sam into looking up and held the coin out in front of her teary eyes.

"Sam, is *this* your bird?"

A look of delight filled the young child's face. "Yes! You found my bird! You found my bird!" She jumped up and down clapping.

"This is why you wanted a birdbath?" Jesse scratched his head, puzzled.

Sam nodded. "It was dirty. I wanted it to take a bath while I was sleeping."

"Where did you find this, Sam?" Jesse asked

"Outside," Sam said quietly.

"Yesterday?" Jesse pressed.

"No..." Sam looked down at her feet. "Before that."

"Why didn't you tell me? This might belong to someone who's missing it," Jesse explained. "That's why we have the lost and found box in the office. You know that's where we keep things we find."

Sam's expression turned stubborn. "But this is my secret."

Paige smiled. "So this is the secret treasure you told me about?"

"Yes." Sam said.

"Are there any more treasures," Paige asked. "Any other birds?"

Sam shook her head. "I've been looking, but I can't find any more."

"Well, we need to keep this, to see who it belongs to," Jesse said, reaching for the coin.

"Not fair! I found it!" Sam's eyes filled with tears again.

Paige intervened. "Sam, I have an idea. Would you like to find out more about your bird? For example, where it came from? And why it was dirty when you found it?"

"I guess so," Sam admitted hesitantly.

"Then we need to take it to someone who will know more about it, to get information."

Sam's mouth turned downward in a pout. "But I don't want you to take it away."

"I have an idea," Paige said, turning to Jesse. "Could we have a pencil and a piece of paper?"

Jesse pulled the requested items out from under the counter and handed them over. Paige set the coin down, eagle side up, and placed the paper over it. She handed the pencil to Sam.

"Here, rub the pencil over the paper. I'll hold the paper for you."

Sam followed the directions, a smile forming as she watched the eagle shape form under the pencil marks.

"Wow, that's cool!"

Paige waited until Sam traced the whole coin and then lifted the paper up, handing it to Sam. "There, now you have a special picture of your bird you can keep while we find out more about it."

"OK," Sam said, pleased but hesitant. "You promise to take care of it?"

"Absolutely," Paige said. "You can be sure we'll take special care of it." Both Jesse and Jake nodded in agreement.

"I'm going to put this up in my room!" Sam took off, one hand holding the paper, the other pulling the back door closed behind her.

"Jesse?" The teacher called from the back room. "We need help with the film, when you get a minute."

"Be right there," Jesse said. He turned back to Paige. "What do you suggest?"

"Rose mentioned at breakfast that there's an appraiser in Silverton. One of her guests went up there to have some coins checked out. I think it's worth a trip."

"It can't hurt," Jake agreed. "And I haven't been on that Durango-Silverton line yet. We could take the train up there to have the coin looked at and bring it right back so you don't have to close the museum."

Jesse paused, but agreed. "See what you can find out. I'd like to know more about it.

"Trust me," Jake laughed. "If you want information, you've got the right girl here." He turned to Paige as Jesse headed to the back room. "OK, let's see if we can keep you out of trouble this time."

CHAPTER ELEVEN

Chancy's Coin Shop sat between a bike repair business and an ice cream parlor, and looked like nothing more than a closet in comparison. The nondescript frontage spanned ten feet at the most, one third of which consisted of the doorway. A sign with faded lettering hung askew from a plastic suction cup and wire. Barred windows filled most of the space to either side of the entrance. The building was badly in need of a paint job. When she saw this less than stellar appearance, Paige's first instinct was to walk away. If Jake hadn't been along for back up, she would have helped herself to a double scoop of butter pecan next door and waited for the train back to Hutchins Creek. But, convinced of safety in numbers, she grabbed Jake's sleeve and stepped through the door.

Inside, the shop seemed even smaller than Paige expected. Cluttered shelves and file cabinets added to the claustrophobic feeling. Dusty boxes teetered one upon another on already crowded countertops. Dim lighting bled through a tattered lampshade on a metal desk in the back corner. Several articles of drab clothing draped over a paint-chipped chair. Paige gripped Jake's arm a little tighter as they approached the old man seated in it.

Chancy Conroy looked as far from a coin appraiser as possible, at least from any stereotype Paige had in her head. He bore the rough complexion of a miner and the wardrobe to go along with it. His hair stuck out at angles that would give Einstein a run for his money. His posture was questionable, too, the way he slouched in his chair, arms draped over the edges, head tilted to one side. He looked about eighty years old, give or take ten years. Paige might have questioned if he was alive had he not suddenly snorted so loudly he rivaled a chugging train.

"Should we wake him?" Paige whispered to Jake, who took a moment to size up the situation. She knew he shared her immediate thoughts. Could this person possibly be the expert Rose recommended? For all Paige knew, he might be a street person who had wandered in, looking for a place to nap. "I don't think this is the right guy," she whispered.

"No, it is," Jake said, pointing to an object in the man's hand. "That's a magnifying loupe. Looks like a good one, too, though it might not be if he drops it while he's sleeping."

They didn't have to decide whether to wake the man. The shrill sound of a phone ringing pierced the air. Paige and Jake both jumped, but not as high as the man in front of them. He shot out of his chair and practically fell face first onto his desk. Miraculously, the loupe remained intact as he dropped it and searched frantically underneath stacks of papers for the phone. By the time he found it, the ringing had stopped.

"Musta not been important," he muttered, as if the phone had only rung three times instead of twelve. "Some people! Can't even give a man time to find his dang phone. Impatient, all these young 'uns these days. Probably those confounded telemarketers, anyway." He sat back down and rubbed his eyes, opening them to look at Paige and Jake as if he'd just noticed them.

"Did you folks just call me?"

Paige couldn't tell if the man was kidding or simply confused. She decided to try a direct approach, figuring they had nothing to lose at this point.

"We heard you might be able to give us some information about a coin we found," Paige ventured.

The man huffed. "Well, if I can't, then nobody can. I've been doing this my whole life. Seen just about every coin ever made here in these United States of America, plus some from around the world. Saw one from Japan once that looked like one 'a them New York rolls, hole in the middle and everything."

"A bagel?" Paige stifled a laugh. Even if they didn't end up with worthwhile information, they were sure to leave Chancy's Coin Shop with a few good stories.

"Yessiree, one of those things. Crazy New Yorkers. Why put a hole in the middle of a perfectly good piece of bread?"

"Why, indeed," Jake chimed in, if only to tease Paige. He shook his head in solidarity with the old man

"So whaddya got to show me? The name's Chancy, by the way."

Paige pulled the gold coin out of her pocket while Chancy sat down, cleared a small space on his desk, and picked up the loupe. She set the coin in front of him and waited while he inspected one side, then the other, then the first side again, then the back one more time. He exhaled loudly, making Paige wonder if he was about to snort like he did earlier. Instead he inhaled again and let out a long, slow whistle.

"Where did you get this?" He looked up at Paige with a focused intensity that seemed to come from another person altogether, not the man who'd been rambling just moments before. He even seemed to have grown younger.

"I..." Paige stalled, instinct telling her not to go into too much detail. They'd come to get information, not to give it. Besides, his sudden change in manner had her on alert.

"She found it," Jake jumped in. "You don't remember where, do you, sweetheart?"

Paige didn't know whether to thank Jake for helping or laugh at his use of the affectionate nickname, which was obviously intended to sidestep Chancy's question. Sweet though it was, this term of endearment was completely out of character for Jake.

"I'm not sure," Paige said. "Somewhere on the ground. Maybe it's from someone's collection and they dropped it?"

Chancy hovered over the coin, studying it more carefully. "Oh, it's from someone's collection, all right. Is this the only coin you found?"

The question caught Paige off guard.

"Yes." She paused, and then repeated the answer more firmly. "Yes, definitely the only one. Do you think there are more like it around?"

"At one point, there would have been almost half a million like it, but gold coins were recalled in 1933 by executive order. Roosevelt made it illegal to hoard the coins. Anything valued over one hundred dollars had to be turned in. A lot of those were melted down."

Chancy sat back, holding the coin in his hand, running his fingers over the surface, as if analyzing the texture. For a fleeting moment, it crossed Paige's mind that he wasn't going to give it back.

"What can you tell us about this coin?" Jake's direct question snapped the man out of his daze.

"It's a Double Eagle, 1926, as you can see. The small 'D' shows it came from the Denver Mint."

Paige leaned forward, trying to get a better look. "Is that the mark below the year?"

Chancy shook his head. "No, those are the initials of the artist, Augustus Saint-Gaudens. The Mint mark is above, located between the second and third numbers."

"And this is all gold, correct?"

"Just about."

"What do you mean?" Paige questioned.

"It's an alloy, ninety percent gold and ten percent copper. That's as pure as you're going to get in a gold coin, little lady. Gotta make 'em strong enough to hold up over time."

"Any idea what it's worth?" Jake asked.

Picking up the loupe, Chancy lifted the coin and squinted through the magnifier. He flipped the coin to the other side, and then turned it sideways to inspect the rim. Deep in concentration, he repeated the steps.

"That would depend on an official grade. You could send it off to the folks at PCGS, but it'll be a month or so before you get it back – sometimes longer, sometimes sooner."

"PCGS?" Paige asked for clarification, though she wasn't about to wait a month for answers.

"Professional Coin Grading Service," Chancy explained. "They'll analyze it and assign a grade, send it back to you securely encapsulated to protect it. That's the official way to go about it. Or...tell you what, I'll buy it now for five hundred dollars."

Jake coughed, which was all the warning Paige needed.

"I'm sorry, Mr. Conroy," Paige said, drumming up a quick excuse around the obvious answer. "But this coin doesn't belong to us. It's not ours to sell. But thank you for the offer, anyway."

"Well, you found it, right? 'Finders keepers' is what they say." Chancy closed his fist around the coin and smiled for the first time, revealing a missing tooth alongside several crooked ones. The smile itself seemed about as straight as the teeth. This convinced Paige that the coin dealer's last name could be shortened to 'Con.'

"Show me where the artist's initials are again?" Paige waited as the old man reluctantly uncurled his fingers and held his palm out with the coin. As he pointed to the area below the year, Paige plucked the coin from his hand, holding it up as if to inspect it. "I see," she said as she stepped away and casually slid the coin back in her pocket.

"You've been very helpful," Jake said, reaching out to shake Chancy's hand.

Paige felt a quiver of nervousness as she watched the two men lock eyes.

"Gosh, I could sure go for a scoop of *dulce de leche*," Paige said.

"Doolchay de what?" Chancy dropped Jake's hand, breaking eye contact with him to shift his attention to Paige.

"Caramel ice cream," Paige explained, reaching for Jake's hand. "Delicious."

Chancy shook his head. "Well, I don't know about any doolchay, but they do have a mighty fine vanilla next door."

"Perfect," Paige said, already halfway to the exit, Jake in tow. "Come on, *sweetheart*," she said to Jake, grinning. "You'll buy me an ice cream, won't you?"

"Of course, *dear*," Jake threw back at Paige as she opened the front door.

"Wait," Chancy called out. "You folks didn't tell me where you're from. Maybe I could contact you if I get more information on your coin."

"Oh," Paige said, just as the door started to close. "We came up from Durango. We're just passing through."

CHAPTER TWELVE

The train's rumbling movement calmed Paige as much as the warmth of Jake's arm around her shoulders did. They were halfway back to Hutchins Creek already, and Paige was only just now beginning to relax. Another half hour and they'd be back at the inn.

"You owe me an ice cream, you know…" As Jake's lips brushed Paige's ear, she raised her head from his chest.

"I know. I just felt too uncomfortable hanging out next door to that coin shop. Something about Chancy Conroy doesn't seem right." Paige accepted a quick kiss and then turned her head toward the window. Tall evergreens and impressive rock formations paraded past the train. The scenery was magnificent, yet Paige remained uneasy.

Jake shook her shoulders gently to encourage her. "I can't say I disagree. At first I thought he was just odd. But he changed when he held the coin, and he didn't seem to want to let it go."

"Exactly what I thought," Paige agreed. "I felt like I had to trick him into giving it back. And I didn't like the way he tried to find out where we were from just as we were leaving. That was strange. He could have asked earlier."

"Yes, he could have," Jake said. "And trying to buy it on the spot for five hundred dollars? That was too fast."

"He never did tell us what he thought it was worth," Paige pointed out.

"Of course not, and he wasn't about to. For one thing, he didn't even bother looking it up. There are price guides for collectibles like that – coins, antiques, baseball cards."

"Are you saying he didn't even care about its value?" Paige looked at Jake, puzzled.

"No," Jake said. "I'm sure he cared. That's his business, buying and selling coins. But something else intrigued him."

"Maybe he thought the coin was a fake." Paige said. "It does look brand new, which is sort of odd for something that old, isn't it?"

Jake shook his head. "He wouldn't have offered that much money if he thought it was fake. And it could look new if it wasn't circulated."

"Well, if it was never circulated, what was it doing on the ground in the middle of a little mountain town?' Paige raised both hands, palms up, as if the answer might drop into them.

"Yoga pose?" Jake teased, earning a playful smack on the shoulder.

Paige settled back against the soft flannel of Jake's shirt. The afternoon trip had been short, but she felt exhausted. She could hardly wait to get back to the inn.

* * *

Henry was waiting by the platform when the train pulled into Hutchins Creek, an unexpected, but welcome sight.

"Rose thought you two might want Lulu to escort you to the inn," Henry said. He hitched his thumb toward the curb, where his pride and joy stood waiting.

"Sounds great," Paige followed Henry to the car. She climbed into the front seat, turned sideways and rested one elbow against the glove compartment.

"She knows Lulu well," Henry said as Jake settled into the back seat. "Lots of quirks to this old girl. Lulu, not Paige," he added quickly.

"Glad you clarified that," Paige laughed. She caught Jake's eye long enough to see him wink at her.

Henry cranked Lulu's engine up and pulled away from the curb.

"That was nice of Rose to send you to pick us up," Paige said. "I'm not sure we even told her we were going."

Henry laughed. "Rose knows everything that goes on in this town, trust me. If anyone knows anything, Rose finds out."

"Then Jesse told her," Paige said, figuring the connection out. "We were at the museum this morning."

"Yep, I heard about that. You found a coin in the yard and went up to Silverton to get it checked out? At least that's what Rose said."

Henry shifted gears, and Lulu jerked. Paige's elbow slipped off the glove compartment, which fell open. She pushed it shut and blocked it.

"Gotta get that fixed," Henry said. He patted the top of the dashboard with one hand. "She's a good ol' car, though." He shifted gears again and settled back in his seat. "So how was your visit to that coin shop? Cantankerous old guy owns it, came around the museum a few times. Hasn't been down here in a while. I think Jesse chased him off because he was rude to some visitors."

"I guess everyone's been around the museum at some point," Paige said.

"Pretty much," Henry agreed. "The museum's a fixture in this area."

"I'd think that would make it more likely people would donate to the restoration fund," Paige said. "If they've been here, they might feel more attached to the project."

Henry nodded. "You'd think so." He was silent a moment. "Seems like donations are slow to come in, though, at least from what Jesse tells me."

Paige noticed that Henry didn't mention that money had been disappearing. Since she only knew this because she'd been eavesdropping, she stayed silent. A few minutes later, Henry pulled up in front of the inn.

"Thanks for the ride," Paige said, hopping out of the car before either Henry or Jake could open the door for her. As much as she appreciated traditional courtesies, she yearned to get inside so she could think about what had happened during the day.

"Anytime. I'll be back around later. Rose is cooking up a big roast, and I don't plan on missing out." Henry waved and drove away.

A fresh pot of coffee was in the lobby when Paige and Jake stepped into the inn. Without hesitating, Jake poured two mugs and handed one to Paige. He nodded toward the front door and Paige took the cue, following him out to the gazebo. Settled in on a wicker love seat with garden-print cushions, they sipped coffee and discussed what they'd learned.

"Well, Paige," Jake said, "I'm not sure how you manage to find intrigue everywhere you go, but at least this time I'm along for the ride. You came here to write about railroading in the Old West, but end up with a mysterious coin, and a few interesting characters."

Paige shrugged. "I think there's always more to stories than what's on the surface. I just like to find out the secrets inside these small towns."

Jake laughed. "Saying you 'just like to find out' is an understatement. I don't think you can stand unanswered questions." He shook his head at her expected frown. "I'm not saying that's a bad thing. After all, you are a reporter. The more you learn, the more you have to report. I didn't understand it before. Now I'm getting more of an idea how that works."

"And how is that," Paige asked.

Jake sipped his coffee, pondering his response. "It simply happens, from what I can see. One thing leads to another. You're curious and persistent."

Paige wrapped her hands around her coffee mug, but said nothing.

"I'm not saying this is a bad thing," Jake said.

Still Paige didn't respond.

"OK," Jake admitted. "Maybe you get into trouble sometimes, but your intentions are good, and you do come up with great stories." He paused, considering Paige's expression. "I'm not gaining any brownie points, am I?"

"Not really."

Jake sighed, set his coffee down on the gazebo's small center table, and wrapped his arms around Paige, pulling her closer as she held her coffee mug out to avoid spilling the hot beverage on them both.

"I just worry about you, that's all." Jake kissed the top of Paige's head, and turned her face toward him with a soft caress of her cheek. He kissed her softly, then took the mug from her hand and set it on the table next to his. Returning to the kiss, he deepened its intensity. Paige felt herself melt into the cushions as she reciprocated his affection. All thoughts of railroads, museums and coins faded from her mind.

"You know, we *are* in the front yard," Paige whispered.

"Are you implying we might need more privacy?"

Paige smiled as her lips trailed along Jake's neck, breathing in his skin's familiar scent, fresh and soothing. It surrounded her with a feeling of safety. She'd never felt as content or alive as she did when in his arms.

"I think that's an excellent idea." Playfully, she pulled away, picked up both coffee mugs and headed for the house, Jake just a few feet behind her.

* * *

"A mighty fine roast, Rose." Henry crossed his fork and knife on his plate in surrender.

"I second that," Jesse said.

"And I third it," Stephen Porter added.

"Auntie Rose is the best cook in the whole world," Sam said.

Paige joined in with her own words of appreciation. "It's so kind of you to include us."

Rose laughed. "Well, you can't eat at The Iron Horse every night. And I enjoy cooking. This old house needs to fill up with people sharing a family meal now and then."

"Does that make it a bed and dinner instead of a bed and breakfast?"

Paige smiled at the Porter son's logic. "I think that makes it a bed and breakfast and sometimes dinner," she said.

"That's right," Tommy said. "But not lunch. We eat lunch at the Rails Café. Or sometimes we go on picnics. Right, Dad?"

"Sometimes I go on picnics with you," Sam said.

Stephen nodded. "That's right, you two. Sometimes we all go on picnics."

"A picnic sounds like a good idea," Paige said. She looked at Jake, who nodded as he cleaned his plate of a last bite of roast.

"Creekside Park is only a few blocks past the museum," Rose offered. "Rails Café makes box lunches. You could pick a couple up tomorrow and spend the afternoon in the park. The creek runs right through it. Nice and peaceful there."

"You should go," Tommy said. "There are turtles in the creek. They're cool."

"And fish," Sam added.

"Sounds like a great recommendation," Paige said. "Maybe we'll do that tomorrow. I have some research to do in the morning, but the afternoon should work."

"It's always good to take breaks," Rose pointed out in true motherly fashion. "All work and no play doesn't do anyone a bit of good,"

"Speaking of work," Stephen said as he turned to Jesse. "How are things going with The Morning Star restoration project? I didn't have a chance to ask you when we stopped by."

"It's coming along," Jesse answered shortly. Paige thought he sounded evasive, as if he wasn't eager for others to know about the slow progress, much less the undesirable steps backwards.

"Well, good," Stephen said, oblivious to Jesse's reluctance to expand on the topic. "That model inside is so attractive. We can hardly wait to see the original car outside looking just as refined."

"It'll look spiffy when it's done," Henry agreed. "Don't you think so, Tommy?"

The young Porter boy nodded. "Spiffy," he repeated. "I like that word, 'spiffy.'"

"Well, now, that's because it's a spiffy word," Henry said.

Rose cleared plates, refusing Paige's help. "You're a guest," she admonished. "You're not allowed to do chores." She chuckled as she took the plates to the kitchen and returned with a peach pie. The guests applauded as she cut slices and passed them around the table.

"None for me, thank you," Paige said. "I'm too full after that wonderful meal, Rose. I couldn't eat another bite."

"I'll have your slice and mine, too!" Tommy's face lit up at the thought.

"You'll have your slice only," Stephen said. "No stomach aches for you tonight."

"Aw, all right."

"I'm going to pass, too, but I'll take a rain check," Jake said. "It looks delicious."

"No crime being too full for dessert," Rose laughed. "I take that as a compliment."

"You should," Jesse said, standing up. "Thanks for another great meal, Rose." He hugged his sister and headed out with Sam. Henry thanked Rose and followed Jesse. Tommy and Stephen left for an after dinner walk, what Rose called a Porter family tradition.

"A quiet evening in?" Jake smiled at Paige.

"Sounds good to me."

CHAPTER THIRTEEN

"You up...for a... field trip?"

Paige leaned over as she spoke, hands on her knees, catching her breath from her morning run. Dressed in old leggings, a torn sweatshirt and perspiring like a gym rat, she knew she wasn't in any shape to head anywhere. But she could take a fast shower and towel dry her hair in time to get on the road.

"Field trip? Aren't we already on one?"

Jake folded the local morning paper and set it down beside his coffee. Just seeing him waiting on the front porch was enough to take away what little breath Paige had left after her run.

"The...altitude here...is over 9,300 feet, right?" Paige panted.

"Yep," Jake quipped. "A good 3,000 feet higher than Jackson Hole. Just think how much easier it will be to run there."

Paige smiled at yet another attempt to convince her to move west. She had a good idea what her answer would be, but wasn't ready to end Jake's wondering. A little suspense couldn't hurt, right?

"I'll take Manhattan any day for an easy morning run."

"Even with taxis trying to run you over?"

"I'm very adept at dodging them," Paige protested. "I have years of practice. I can dodge pretzel vendors, too."

"Pretzel vendors?"

"Never mind," Paige laughed. "What do you say to the field trip?"

"You expect me to agree without even knowing where we're going?

Paige tapped a finger against her lip. "Would you agree? It would be an adventure."

"No doubt, with you in the lead," Jake laughed.

"And...it will be an overnight adventure. Pack your bag. I'll tell Rose we'll be away tonight, so she won't worry."

Before Jake could answer, Paige disappeared inside the inn, headed for the shower. In less than an hour, they were on the road.

"Are you going to tell me where we're going?" Jake glanced at Paige as he drove out of Hutchins Creek. "'Turn left and head north' isn't quite enough for me to go on."

Paige propped her feet up against the dashboard and fumbled with a map. After turning it several times, she settled it across her legs and traced a route with her index finger.

"I'm thinking north to Interstate 70 and then east..." She paused. "No, maybe cutting across Highway 50 is better. Looks a little shorter. What do you think?"

"I think it would be easier for me to answer if you told me where we were going."

Paige looked up and smiled. "Denver."

"Denver?" Jake exclaimed. "That's a good six hours from here."

"Well, I did say it was an overnight trip. It's only mid-morning. We'll be there before dinner."

"OK, I give up. What's in Denver?"

Paige looked out the window, avoiding Jake's quick glances in her direction. "Well, for one thing, the Colorado Railroad Museum is just outside Denver. It's much larger than the museum in Hutchins Creek. They may have additional information Jesse can't offer."

"Paige, I know you too well," Jake said. "You're looking the other direction while you're telling me this, so I know you've got something else up your sleeve. Might as well confess."

"A romantic overnight escape doesn't quite cut it?"

"Nope. We're already on one of those." Jake said. "So, spill it."

Paige sighed. "OK. I sent an email to the Denver Mint yesterday after we got back from Silverton."

"Don't tell me…"

"I had an email from them this morning, before I went running. They give tours; we can take one tomorrow morning." Paige's voice grew more animated as she explained. "And I figure someone will be able to look at the coin and give us more information about it." She patted her hip, where the gold coin was safely pocketed. "We can take the tour, ask about the coin, and get back to Hutchins Creek by tomorrow night."

"How did I not see this coming?" Jake fought back a smile, unsuccessfully.

"I knew you wouldn't mind," Paige whispered, leaning over to kiss Jake's shoulder before scooting closer to place another kiss on his neck.

"Careful," Jake said, grinning. "I'm trying to watch the road."

"Gotcha," Paige agreed, looking back at the map. "Kind of glad to hear I'm a distraction, though." She smiled and shot him a sideways look.

"You have no idea," Jake laughed. Reaching over with one hand, he squeezed the back of Paige's neck. She dropped her head forward, enjoying the strength of his fingers on her muscles for a few seconds before he let go to keep both hands on the wheel. She rested her head back against the seat and closed her eyes.

* * *

"Where are we?"

Paige lifted her head, glancing first out the window and then at Jake. She hadn't intended to doze off, but the movement of the vehicle, along with the soothing feeling of Jake's presence, had lulled her into a short nap. Or was it short?

"Well, hello there, Rip Van MacKenzie," Jake said. "To answer your question, we're about two hours outside of Denver."

"Seriously? I've been asleep for four hours?" Paige sat up and stretched her arms as much as was possible within the confined space. She rubbed her eyes and ran her fingers through her disheveled hair. Pulling down the visor, she took a peek in the mirror, shrugged and flipped the visor back up. All things considered, she could look worse. Her freshly washed hair from the morning shower looked windswept and natural. Her green T-shirt matched her eyes. She hadn't even lost one of her silver earrings while she slept, though a line on the side of her face showed she'd had her head pressed against the seat for much of the trip.

"You look as beautiful as ever," Jake said.

"Thanks. But you'd say that whether it were true or not."

"Maybe," Jake admitted. "But it happens to be true." He paused. "Just as true as all those things you said in your sleep..."

"What?" Paige shook her head. "I don't talk in my sleep."

"Sure you do," Jake continued. "Something about a handsome cowboy and a big ranch and..."

"OK, I get the picture," Paige laughed. "I'm pretty sure I don't talk in my sleep, but I admit I do dream about you sometimes."

"Really? Do tell," Jake said, relaxing against the seat, a smug look on his face.

"Well, let me see..." Paige said slowly, as if she were trying to remember details. "Usually you're walking briskly along a sidewalk in Manhattan, dressed in a suit, glancing at your watch, worrying about being late to your Wall Street job."

"Seriously?"

Paige smiled at Jake's horrified look. She'd concocted what she knew would be his worst nightmare. "Of course not," she laughed.

They fell into a comfortable silence. Jake focused on navigating winding roads while Paige admired the Rocky Mountain scenery flowing by, lost in her own thoughts. Portions of the visit to the coin shop kept popping into her head – the strange expression on Chancy Conroy's face when he saw the coin, his attempt to find out where they were from just as they were leaving. She always trusted her instincts, and they told her there was a story behind the old man's reaction to their visit. Which translated to a story about the coin. From the moment they met the old man, she had no doubt he was odd. But he changed into something more when he saw the coin.

"He knows more about it than he's saying," Paige mumbled, half to herself.

"What? Are you talking in your sleep again?"

"Ha. No, I'm just thinking that Chancy Conroy knows more about that 1926 Double Eagle than he let on when we were there, beyond the basic details he explained. I think he knows its story."

"You can't be sure, Paige," Jake said. "He's obviously eccentric. He might have just been excited to see that particular coin. Maybe he has a collection with all but that one in it. Or he might have a buyer who's been looking for a Double Eagle from that year. He certainly was eager to buy it."

"That's true," Paige said. "And I don't doubt he was eager to buy it. But I'm telling you there's something more going on."

"Your hunches are usually right, I admit."

"Then I say we get into Denver, find dinner and a comfortable place for the night. And we'll see what the Denver Mint has to say about our eagle in the morning."

CHAPTER FOURTEEN

Paige leaned against the wall outside the Cherokee Street entrance to the Denver Mint, blowing across her vanilla latte to cool it down.

"We really had to be here this early?" Jake held his own coffee, strong and black with "none of that fancy stuff," as he'd described it when he ordered.

"Yes," Paige said, not for the first time that morning. "We were lucky to get the eight o'clock tour as it is, thanks to a cancellation. They're booked all week. And we're required to be here thirty minutes early."

"Which explains why we're here just a few minutes after seven?"

"Better early than late," Paige said, watching Jake yawn. She knew he wasn't complaining, that he was just giving her a hard time. The basic, but convenient lodging they'd taken for the previous night was close by. It had been easy to be on time for the early tour. "Besides, we have a long drive to get back to Hutchins Creek later today, so the earlier we take the tour the better."

"True," Jake said. "Plus, you said you want to swing by the Colorado Railroad Museum on the way out."

"Exactly." Paige sipped her hot beverage and gave Jake a sweet smile. "A whirlwind trip, right? Exciting."

"Sure," Jake quipped. "Seven hundred round trip miles of excitement."

"Beautiful scenery, though," Paige pointed out.

"I can't argue with that. I've always loved the Rocky Mountains," Jake admitted. He downed the rest of his coffee and threw the empty cup in a nearby trashcan. "Glad these are biodegradable. Can't take them inside, you know."

Paige nodded. "I know. Small wallet in one pocket and cell phone – turned off – in the other. That's it. I read up on the rules when I made the reservation." She finishing her latte and threw her cup in the can after Jake's.

"Can't blame them for not wanting backpacks or purses inside," Jake said.

"Absolutely," Paige agreed as she watched others arrive, including the guide, who checked names and confirmation numbers before starting the tour.

"The Denver Mint has been producing coins at this location since 1906." The guide, a middle-aged gentleman with short, brown hair and wire-rimmed glasses, looked a bit like a university professor. He gave a brief history of the building and process of coin production, and the detailed descriptions he offered convinced Paige that their guide, Edward Ferguson, was the right source for information. She followed along throughout the facility as he explained the steps of blanking, annealing, upsetting and striking the coins. Although her primary goal was to learn more about the specific coin in her pocket, the tour fascinated her.

"It never occurred to me that so much went into making coins," Paige said to Jake as the group disbursed to hunt for souvenirs in the gift shop.

"I never thought about it, either," Jake said. He lifted a commemorative set off a display, admiring the presentation.

"I'll be right back," Paige whispered, taking off before Jake could ask where she was headed. Edward Ferguson had just finished answering a question from another tour member.

"Mr. Ferguson," Paige said, catching him just as he was turning to leave. "I'm Paige MacKenzie. I just took your tour and was hoping to ask a few questions."

"Yes, Ms. MacKenzie." The resigned, yet polite, expression on the guide's face told Paige the normal question and answer period was over. Yet she'd had to wait until the other tour members had moved on in order to speak with him in private.

"It's just Paige. And I'm sorry. I know you've already answered questions. But the tour was wonderful. You're obviously knowledgeable, and I have a specific question."

"Thank you," the guide said, taking off his glasses. Pulling a cloth out of his pocket, he began cleaning one of the lenses. "I'm glad you enjoyed it. I like giving tours, and I've spent my lifetime studying coins. It's my passion, really. I'm happy to answer your question."

Paige looked over her shoulder impulsively, and she realized immediately that the gesture might make it appear as if she were doing something prohibited. She shook off the feeling and turned back to the guide, pulling the coin out of her pocket.

"This is what I wanted to ask you about."

The guide glanced at the coin, squinting.

"Nice replica of a Double Eagle. Those were beautiful coins back in the day. A lot of them got melted down when Roosevelt recalled them."

Paige felt an equal mix of confusion and disappointment. Could it be just a replica? Why would Chancy Conroy have offered five hundred dollars on the spot for the coin? Either the appraiser didn't know what he was talking about, or the guide was confused.

"Yes, I've heard a little about that," Paige said, stalling while the guide moved the cloth to the other lens. Finished with cleaning, he placed the glasses squarely on the bridge of his nose and took another look at the coin, this time more closely. His eyebrows rose in surprise. He nodded toward the gift shop and walked that way, Paige following closely behind.

"Louise, let me see that loupe you've got on hand."

The gift shop clerk, a spry senior citizen, reached below the counter and pulled out the now-familiar magnification tool. "Now, don't you go forgetting you borrowed that, Fergie."

Paige smiled at the clerk's use of a nickname for the guide.

"Let's go look at this coin a little closer," Ferguson said. He headed to a doorway in the far corner of the gift shop. Paige waved at Jake and motioned for him to join them.

The modest back room was approximately twelve by fifteen feet, large enough for several shelves of reference books and a rectangular table in the center. A variety of work tools spread across the table: a microscope, several lamps, an assortment of magnifying glasses, small bottles of liquid, and a tray filled with cotton gloves. Paige wasn't sure if the paraphernalia made her feel more hopeful or just nervous. She reached for Jake's hand, glad that he'd followed her into the room.

"Don't let all this stuff intimidate you," Ferguson said. "The equipment helps us identify coins."

"Well, as you suggested when you first saw the coin, I know this is a Double Eagle. It's dated 1926 and that 'D' means it was made in Denver. It's gold, mostly. Ninety percent gold and ten percent copper, I believe." Paige straightened up, proud of her limited yet accurate knowledge.

"Yes," Ferguson agreed. "You've got the basics down. Sounds like you've done some research. Many people think gold coins are pure gold. Or that silver coins are one hundred percent silver."

"That wouldn't be strong enough, would it?" Paige asked.

"Exactly right," Ferguson said as he slipped his hands into cotton gloves from the nearby tray. "If the coins weren't made of an alloy, they couldn't withstand circulation."

"They don't do too well on railroad tracks as it is," Jake said.

Both Paige and Ferguson sent him disapproving looks.

"So I've heard, anyway," Jake added quickly.

"Where did you get this coin?" Ferguson said. He focused his attention on a microscope, where he'd placed the coin for closer inspection. Turning on a small light mounted on the inside of the neck, he rested his eyes against the equipment's dual eyepieces.

"I found it," Paige said, deciding to stick with the simple answer she'd offered in Silverton. For the second time, she'd been asked where she found the coin before being told anything about it. "On the ground, in the dirt." This, at least, was true.

A moment passed quietly as Ferguson inspected both sides of the coin, as well as the rim.

"Fascinating, isn't it?" Paige said to break the silence.

"Absolutely," Ferguson agreed. He straightened up, pushed away from the microscope, and detached a walkie-talkie from a strap inside his jacket. Holding a button down on the side, he brought the radio to his mouth. "Simons, I have something you'll want to see."

Jake cast a protective glance at Paige and looked at the guide. "Who is Simons?"

Ferguson patted the air with his hand, as if to say not to worry. "Just someone else who works here." He turned to face Paige and Jake, a calm, pleased expression on his face. "I think you folks have a special coin here. I just want to get another opinion."

"Great," Paige said, her enthusiasm growing. This certainly beat the sleazy reaction they'd received in Silverton. Hopefully they were about to get some decent insight.

It only took a minute for the newcomer to arrive.

"What is it, Ferguson?"

Of all the figures Paige might have imagined coming through the doorway, a man in a blue uniform with badge and holstered gun was nowhere on that list. He was broad-shouldered, sturdy and serious.

"Wait a minute," Jake said. "What's going on here?"

"This is Officer Simons," Ferguson said. "He's a member of the U.S. Mint Police. He's a detective. As am I."

"You're a police officer? A detective? Not a guide?" Paige wondered if it were possible to be any more confused than she already was. She'd thought the trip to Silverton was strange, but this experience now far surpassed the visit with Chancy Conroy.

"I fill in as a guide when they're short-handed," Ferguson explained. "Someone called in sick this morning."

Paige nodded as if this information was important to her, though it wasn't.

"Why don't you two take a seat?" Officer Simons said, his expression unreadable. He pointed to two chairs at the table.

Paige and Jake exchanged looks. As they took places at the table, Officer Simons did the same. Ferguson remained where he was, setting the microscope with the coin still in it aside.

"I don't understand what's going on," Paige blurted out. She shook off Jake's arm as he reached out to calm her before she could say anything she might regret. "What exactly have we done wrong?"

"You haven't done anything wrong," Ferguson said. "You're not in trouble. I just wanted Simons here because he'll have questions."

"Right." Simons nodded, though Paige could tell he was just supporting Ferguson. He had no more idea what was going on than she and Jake did.

Ferguson took the coin out from under the microscope and set it on the table.

"I believe this coin is from a batch that was stolen."

"Stolen!" Paige exclaimed, jumping up. "You've got to be kidding…" She paused, noting Officer Simons' stern expression and sat back down. "OK, obviously you aren't kidding. But I…we…have no idea what you're talking about."

"I know that," Ferguson said. "Like I said, you aren't in trouble. Let me explain."

Both Ferguson and Simons' expressions softened. Paige felt slightly relieved, though still uncomfortable enough to cross her arms and chew on her bottom lip.

"I assure you we didn't steal anything," Paige said.

"Obviously not," Ferguson said, holding back a grin. "This happened ninety years ago. That would have been quite a feat for you to pull off."

"So tell us," Jake said.

"Ninety years ago…of course, in 1926," Paige reasoned. "The year the coin was minted."

"Exactly," Officer Simons said. "A small batch went missing."

"Define 'small.'" Jake said.

"Our records show twenty-six pieces," Ferguson said. "That's small enough that someone could walk out with them hidden in their clothing."

"I wouldn't think someone could just walk out," Jake said. "Don't you have strict security here? Isn't this where the expression, 'as secure as Fort Knox' comes from?"

"Absolutely correct," Ferguson said.

"That was almost a century ago," Paige pointed out. "Maybe it wasn't as secure then?"

Both officers looked at Paige as if she'd uttered blasphemy. She quickly backtracked. "I mean to say, I'm sure the Mint has always been secure, but maybe the procedures were different back then?"

Officer Ferguson shook his head. "Nothing that would have allowed someone to walk out unnoticed. That's why we've always known it had to be an inside job."

"An inside job?" Paige asked. She leaned forward, forearms against the table, her curiosity growing.

"Someone inside the building at the time," Ferguson continued. "An employee may have pulled it off. Or he could have turned a blind eye when the theft occurred, expecting to get cut in on the deal. Who knows? The authorities suspected one guard in particular, but an investigation led nowhere. He was cleared."

"And they never found any of the coins?" Paige asked.

"Not until now," Officer Simons said. "Which is why it's important you tell us where you found this."

"And 'in the dirt' isn't quite enough," Ferguson added.

Paige sighed. "I found it behind the railroad museum in Hutchins Creek. And it *was* in the dirt. That's truly all I know." She paused. "Are you sure this isn't a replica after all?"

"Almost positive," Ferguson said. "But we'll do more testing to be sure."

"I take it we're leaving it with you?" Paige sighed. "This will make a certain little girl very unhappy." She told the officers the story about Sam and her "bird."

"I have an idea," Ferguson said. He left the room and returned shortly with a replica coin from the gift shop. "It's a different year, but otherwise looks exactly the same. I think this 'bird' will do the trick."

"Thanks," Paige said. "A great idea. Let me pay you for this."

"Not necessary," Officer Simons smiled. "I suspect we got the better end of the deal."

"If it checks out the way you think it will, I'd say you're right," Jake agreed.

After a few formalities and exchanges of names and phone numbers, Ferguson and Simons escorted Paige and Jake to the exit.

"Thanks for your help," Ferguson said, shaking Paige's hand. "I'm sorry to blindside you like that. I'd also like to ask you to keep this quiet and not to pursue it on your own."

"Of course," Paige said, causing Jake to cough.

"Water?" Ferguson pointed to a drinking fountain in the hallway.

"No, no, I'm fine," Jake insisted as Paige elbowed him.

Paige turned back to the officers just before they pulled the door closed.

"Just one last question, officers," she asked. "Do either of you know the name of the guard who was cleared?"

Ferguson scratched his head and looked at Officer Simons. "Fred? Or was it Frank?"

Officer Simons' brow furrowed. "I don't recall."

"It was Frank, I think…" Ferguson finally said. "Yes, his name was Frank Conroy."

CHAPTER FIFTEEN

Paige looked out the window. The long drive, the surprising discovery at the Denver Mint, and their stop at the Colorado Railroad Museum, had all taken their toll on her, and she could barely keep her eyes open. Yet she juggled too many thoughts to be able to sleep.

"What time is it?" Paige leaned over to check the clock in the dashboard and answered her own question. "Four o'clock. How much longer?"

"We're still a couple of hours away from Hutchins Creek." Jake said. "About twenty minutes closer than the last time you asked. Those two full hours we spent at the railroad museum definitely stretched the day out."

"True, but that was important for my work. I need to type out my outlines and send them to Susan to see which angle she prefers. Besides, I wanted to learn more about the Denver-Rio Grande line. I have a feeling the story behind this coin and the railroad history might tie together."

Jake shot Paige a quick glance. "How is that?"

Paige turned sideways and rested her left elbow on the seat back. "You remember when Rose first told us about the Hutchins family, about each generation going back?"

"You mean the ones where they forgot to name someone 'Jake'?"

"Very funny," Paige sighed, too tired to laugh.

"Yes, I remember," Jake said. "They all worked for the railroad, even the original Hutchins who founded the town."

Paige nodded. "Right. But a couple did odd jobs, too, remember?"

"You're right. Which ones?"

"Jasper and Jerome, I think," Paige said. "Jesse's grandfather and father. Jed's son and grandson."

"Well, I'm glad you have that straight, because I sure don't." Jake braked abruptly to let a deer cross the road, and then breathed a sigh of relief. "I'm glad it's still light out. This wouldn't be an easy drive at night."

"Jed, Jasper, Jerome, Jesse." Paige recited the chronological order of Hutchins men.

"It just sounds like a tongue twister to me," Jake said. "Speaking of names, what about the guard back then? Frank Conroy? It's awfully coincidental that he and that coin dealer share a last name."

"I agree. Frank Conroy? Chancy Conroy? They could definitely be related. Odd that Chancy never mentioned a family connection with the Mint, though."

Jake shook his head, but kept his eyes on the road. "Doesn't strike me as odd at all. Think about it, Paige. That guard was involved in a scandal. Why would a relative offer that information upfront, especially to people he'd just met? I wouldn't start a conversation with that."

"Makes sense," Paige admitted. "And once he saw the coin, he wasn't about to say anything." She paused. "But if he and Frank are related, that would explain why he acted so strangely once he saw the coin. It also explains why he didn't want to give it back."

"Sounds like someone with a guilty conscience, don't you think, Paige?"

"Yes, but I think it's more complicated than that. Obviously Chancy isn't the guard who worked there. He's too young."

"So he's the son of that guard," Jake said. "Or maybe even the grandson."

"Let's see," Paige calculated. "That was ninety years ago. So if Frank Conroy worked there in his twenties, and Chancy was born when Frank was in his forties, that would make Chancy around seventy now."

"Sounds about right."

Paige nodded. "He looked around that age, maybe a little older. One thing is certain: Chancy didn't take the coins. But his father could have."

"If they're related, that is," Jake pointed out.

"Exactly." Paige rubbed her temples, feeling a dull headache coming on. "But Ferguson and Simons, the detectives, said Frank Conroy was cleared."

"Doesn't mean he didn't do it," Jake said. "But that would be quite a caper to pull off without getting caught."

"Well, he *was* the guard. It might have been easier for him to get away with the theft than for someone else," Paige said. "Anyone else would have had to pass by him in order to get out."

"He couldn't have been the only guard," Jake said. "Not for a place that big and that important. Maybe several guards were in on it together split the coins up afterwards."

"Maybe."

Paige closed her eyes and leaned back against the head rest, silent. Everything was conjecture at this point. The only solid fact was that coins went missing that year. Who took them and how they managed it were questions with dozens of possible answers. They weren't even certain the coin found behind the Hutchins Creek Museum came from that batch of stolen coins. If it did, why weren't there more? Or were there? She made a mental note to ask Sam if she'd found any other "birds" yet.

By the time they reached Silverton, Paige had formed a half dozen theories, some logical, some not. If Sam's coin *was* from the stolen batch, someone might have hidden it in the museum yard temporarily. Or any visitor to the museum, a stranger who found it elsewhere, could have dropped it. Chancy could even have done it, for that matter, though Frank and Chancy might not even be related. Conroy was a common enough name. Which just meant Chancy was a weird, old man, not a thief – or descendant of a thief. The possibilities were endless.

"Pull off here," Paige said, pointing to an exit.

"Really, Paige? I don't think going to the coin shop again is a good idea. And we've only got another hour to go. Don't you want to get back to the inn to relax? And aren't you hungry? It's already past seven."

"I'm sure Chancy's shop is closed," Paige pointed out. "But the ice cream parlor might be open. Maybe they serve sandwiches." She turned to Jake and gave him one of her more pleading looks.

"You expect me to believe you simply want to visit the ice cream shop? Or have a sandwich for dinner?"

"Why not?"

Jake laughed. "Because I've known you for almost a year now, and you wanting to stop by a place that's *next to* a location involving one of your mysteries is never random."

"Maybe I just feel like that butter pecan we didn't get last time."

"Nice try, but not buying it."

Paige sighed. "OK, I just want to look, maybe drive around the block. Humor me. It'll only take a few minutes. It's not that much out of our way."

Given Jake's hesitance, Paige was surprised when he actually took the exit. Inwardly, she patted herself on the back for convincing him. She'd always had a knack for charming people into doing things, a trait with both positive and negative repercussions. She scooted closer to him and thanked him with a sweet kiss on the cheek.

It took only a couple of minutes to locate Chancy's store again, which was, as they expected, closed. But the ice cream parlor was open.

"You're not really going to have ice cream this close to dinner, are you?"

Paige laughed. "Now you're my dad? No, I'm not. I'd love to take some to Rose, but it would melt before we get there. How about popping in for coffee, just for five or ten minutes, and then getting back on the road?"

"I can go for that," Jake said. "A little caffeine before those last miles isn't a bad idea."

Jake parked the car in front of the ice cream parlor and escorted Paige inside. A dozen customers sat at old-fashioned tables in the '50s style interior. Shelving held nostalgic items such as vintage toys, mason jars and kitchen gadgets. Metal Coca-Cola signs and kitchen utensils filled other wall spaces. A gum ball machine stood near the front door.

As the counter clerk began to take their order, Paige asked for coffee with light cream and sugar, plus "whatever he'd like." Before Jake could say a word, she added, "Be right back. Grab us a table," and she slipped out the front door. Without even looking back, she knew Jake was shaking his head at her ploy to get away.

Although she was tempted to peek in the front windows of the coin shop, Paige ruled it out. She had no reason to believe anyone would be watching her, but it seemed too risky a move. Noting a narrow space between the two buildings, she turned sideways and wriggled her way through until she emerged into a back alley. Shaking off claustrophobia from the tight passageway, she took a deep breath and looked around.

Both buildings had rear parking spaces. A newer economy car sat behind the ice cream parlor, fitting with the image of the college-aged clerk. A dusty vehicle that had to be older than Paige filled a space behind the coin shop. Although multiple layers of dirt made identifying the color difficult, tan was her best guess. She stepped around it, trying not to brush up against the filthy metal, approached a window at the rear of the shop and pressed up against the glass.

The dim interior of Chancy's shop wasn't much to look at. Wooden cabinets lined the walls, most with narrow drawers much smaller than one might use for clothing or tools. Stacks of papers covered the floor. An overflowing trash can sat to one side of a worktable. A wall divider approximately ten feet from where Paige stood separated the back area from the front of the shop, making it impossible to see where she and Jake had stood during their previous visit. It didn't matter. Now that she'd seen both the front of the shop and the back, she didn't see much of note.

Paige whirled around at the sound of a slow whistle to find Jake. His attention wasn't on her, but on the dusty car. He held two paper cups of coffee.

"Nice '63 Impala," Jake said, admiring the vehicle. "The owner ought to fix this up."

"That old thing? It looks ready for the junk yard, if you ask me." Paige turned her head sideways, as if a different angle might make the car more appealing somehow.

"You just don't know your classic cars," Jake said, circling the Impala.

"Never were high on my interest list. And you don't know how to grab a table and wait for me," Paige teased lightly, hoping to diffuse the inevitable conversation.

"Yes, speaking of which," Jake's tone became more serious. "Did you really think I'd fall for that trick? I got the coffee to go and followed you as fast as I could. Would have been here sooner if I hadn't had to walk around to the alley. Did you squeeze through that passage between the buildings?"

"Yes, barely."

"You could have gotten stuck."

Paige glared him.

"Not the right thing to say?"

"No."

"I meant that anyone could get stuck in there."

"I know what you meant," Paige said. "Anyway, we can go. We'll drink the coffee on the way back to the inn."

"Learn anything here?" Jake asked.

"Only that whoever owns that car needs to wash it."

Paige took the coffee cup Jake held out. They followed the alley around to the main street and returned to Jake's truck, where they climbed in and set the coffee cups in the drink holders.

As Jake pulled away from the curb, Paige took one last look back at Chancy's Coin Shop. For a brief second, she thought she saw movement inside the front window. But the early evening shadows on other windows were identical. She brushed off the idea and settled back for the final miles to Hutchins Creek.

CHAPTER SIXTEEN

Sam clapped her hands as Paige pulled the replica coin from her pocket and handed it over. The little girl jumped up and down then ran out the museum's back door and immediately placed the coin in the birdbath, now firmly replanted in the yard. She then skipped in circles, bright sunlight dancing through her blond curls. Her pink ruffled skirt lifted up and down in the light summer breeze with each hop.

Paige smiled. Just as she'd hoped, Sam didn't notice the different year stamped on the coin; the detectives were right when they suggested the substitution would work. Sam was simply happy to have the coin back. That was all that mattered.

"You sure made Sam one happy girl today," Jesse said. "She loves that 'bird.'" He finished sticking prices on the back of a short stack of coloring books, turned the stack right-side-up and carried it to a rack in the book section. After he straightened the display, he returned to the main counter. "How did your trip go? Rose said you were hoping to get more information about the coin. Did The Denver Mint have anything to say about it?"

"Did they ever," Paige started to fill Jesse in, but abruptly changed direction. "Wait, I meant to ask you something as soon as I came in today, but Sam's joy at getting back her coin distracted me."

"What did you want to ask me? I'm happy to oblige," Jesse waved to a young couple wandering in then turned back to Paige.

"I was just wondering if Sam has mentioned finding any other birds." Paige watched Jesse take his time processing her question.

"You mean coins? Not that I can recall," he said. "Hard to tell sometimes, though. The child's imagination sometimes makes it hard for *me* to tell what's real." He laughed.

"Yes," Paige laughed. "I can see that."

"What makes you think there might be more?" Jesse asked.

Paige was surprised at her reluctance to answer. She'd planned to fill Jesse in on the information about the stolen coins, but something told her to hold back. Did she suspect he might be involved? That was absurd. He was far too young to have had anything to do with the theft itself. But...that didn't keep him from knowing what went on in previous generations.

"Just curious," Paige said. "They minted close to a half million that year. It makes sense a few more might be around where one was found."

Jesse shook his head. "We would have found them by now. We've done a lot of work out there in the yard. I'm surprised Sam found the one she did. I wish we could ask Grandpa Jasper, but he's long gone, died back in 1969. He'd probably know something about the coin. He worked at the Denver Mint for a few years."

"I thought he was a railroad man?" Paige could barely get the question out, stunned as she was at the new information.

"He was, for many years. But he started out working different jobs. Maybe didn't want to follow in his father's footsteps. You know how kids can be rebellious as teenagers."

"Sure," Paige said.

"Or maybe he was just heartbroken. He married his first wife young, at just eighteen. A year later he lost his bride when the Spanish Flu Epidemic hit. Wiped out ten percent of

Silverton's population, that flu. That's when he took off for Denver."

Jesse answered the ringing phone, gave out the operating hours of the museum, and hung up with a cheerful "we hope to see you." Changing subjects, he asked. "Where's your friend today?"

"Oh, Jake? He decided to get some work done on his business and stayed at the inn while I came to see Sam. Either that or he wanted more of Rose's pancakes."

"I can understand that," Jesse said. "Rose managed to pick up the cooking gene from our mother."

"She was a good cook?" Paige welcomed a chance to talk about Hutchins family history.

"The best," Jesse insisted. "You'll never find a pie crust as flaky as hers, or a roast with such perfect spices. She knew what she was doing in the kitchen. You can't imagine the family dinners we used to have."

"Tell me about them," Paige said, leaning on the counter.

Jesse excused himself to hand a museum brochure to the young couple, who were headed out to the back yard.

"Sunday evenings were the big draw," Jesse said as he returned to the counter. "I remember those meals back to when I was just a boy. Mom would cook up a feast and no one in the family would miss it. Dad was there, of course, along with a few of his friends who just 'happened to stop by.' As if everyone in town didn't already know the Hutchins house was the best place for a Sunday meal. Mom always cooked huge portions, way more than just the family could eat. Hard to know if she cooked that much knowing people would come over or if people came over knowing there'd be that much food."

"Sounds like good times," Paige said.

"Great times," Jesse said. "Grandpa Jasper was still alive when I was young. Boy, did he ever love Mom's meat loaf. That and potatoes, mashed but still lumpy. He must have put four tablespoons of butter on one serving of those potatoes. Pearl used to scold him something awful."

"Pearl?"

"My grandmother," Jesse explained. "Jasper's second wife. She was always the reasonable one. Grandpa lived on the edge, but she kept him under control. All except that butter, that is," Jesse laughed. "She never won that battle. Jasper was proud of it, too."

"You must miss your grandparents."

"They were fun to be around growing up," Jesse said. "I still visit Grandma Pearl when I can. I should go more often." He popped open the cash drawer and broke out a roll of quarters, letting them fall into the tray like a cascading metal waterfall.

"Is she buried in a local cemetery?" Paige said. "I visit my grandparents where they're resting on the East Coast."

"Oh, no," Jesse shook his head. "Pearl's still alive, down in an assisted care facility in Durango. One hundred and one years old on her last birthday, can you believe it? She even makes sense some days. Has her confused days, too."

"Wow, that's certainly understandable. That means she was born in…" Paige paused to do the math.

"Nineteen fifteen," Jesse said. "She was younger than Jasper, who was born in 1905."

"Ten years, not that many, really," Paige said. "I know couples with similar age differences who have great marriages."

"Well, it worked for them, that's for sure. They were quite a team, adored each other. Grandma Pearl still talks about Grandpa – though, like I said, sometimes she makes sense, other times she doesn't. The nurses there call her 'The Bird Lady' because she tends to poke the air with her hands and talk about 'all the pretty birds.' We never know which stories are true and which aren't. But she loves to tell 'em. That's what matters."

"'The Bird Lady,' you say? Like Sam, who talks about her 'bird'?"

"I suppose so," Jesse said. "Maybe this whole family is a little 'cuckoo,' if you know what I mean."

Paige's cell phone rang, so she stepped outside the back door to take the call, expecting it to be Jake. Instead it was Susan, checking progress on the railroad article.

"Great," Paige said. "I'm about to start working on the full article."

Paige had already set the evening aside to go over notes from the Colorado Railroad Museum. Starting on the final article wouldn't be a problem. She'd even allotted time for a meal at The Iron Horse with Jake. They could hit the early bird special before her writing session. Or she could finish up the article and then have a late romantic meal. She smiled at the latter thought. It was definitely the more appealing plan.

"You'll like this one, Susan," Paige added. "The railroad history out here is fascinating. I took photos at the museum outside Denver yesterday, too. I'll send high-resolution images along with the copy. Say hi to everyone in the office."

Paige disconnected the call and turned her attention to Sam, who'd been playing on the ground underneath The Morning Star. As expected, the child emerged covered in dirt. Paige smiled. Clean or dirty, the young waif was enchanting.

"Find anything interesting?" Paige called out.

"Nope," Sam replied. She brushed her hands against each other and returned to the birdbath.

"How's your bird doing?" Paige walked closer.

"Fine. He's clean now." Sam patted down her skirt, which did nothing to clean off the dirt. Paige suspected it would find its way into a washing machine that evening.

"Have you found any other birds out here?" Paige asked.

"Nope." Sam shrugged, removed the coin from the birdbath and dried it off with her skirt. Examining it closely, she determined it wasn't clean enough and dropped it back into the water.

The soft chime of bells from her phone blended perfectly with the wind. The call was from Jake this time.

"How're the business calls going?" Paige said.

"Great, actually," Jake said. "I've got a good lead on some used horse fencing and a couple of experienced workers to put it in."

"That's nice…" Paige said hesitantly. "Except for one tiny detail – you don't have any horses."

"True," Jake laughed.

"So am I missing something?" Paige watched Sam emerge from the house. She looked over to make sure Paige was watching before running back to the museum yard.

"Probably," Jake said. "Why don't we talk about it over a nice dinner at The Iron Horse?"

"Exactly what I was thinking," Paige agreed. "I just have to draft some of that article first. I promised Susan I would. And I don't think I'll feel like working on it after dinner."

"No, I don't think you will." Jake's smile came through in his voice. Paige felt a jolt of excitement run through her. The man had no idea what kind of effect he caused, the way she lost her breath just thinking of being around him. Still, work first. The email to her editor was non-negotiable.

"Let me finish up here, say goodbye to Sam and Jesse. I'll come back to work on the article at the inn – by myself," Paige added.

"Collaborating might be more fun," Jake hinted.

"Collaborating might mean missing a deadline," Paige countered. "I'll work in the front parlor or out at the gazebo if the wind settles down."

"Anything new at the museum?"

"Not really," Paige said. "Sam's happy to have the coin back."

"I take it she didn't notice it was a substitution."

"No, it passed the switch test just fine. She ran right out to bathe it."

"Does this give new meaning to the term, 'laundering money'?"

"I imagine so," Paige laughed. She ended the call and slid the phone back in her pocket as she walked over to the birdbath.

"Look how shiny it is now!" Sam waved the coin in the air. "It just needed another bath."

"It looks great!" Paige found the girl's enthusiasm contagious, a reminder that simple things can be more important than they seem. Children understood this. One shiny coin made Sam's morning complete.

Then again, that had been Sam's goal. Paige often set goals that were a bit more complicated. For example, finding out how a Double Eagle from a ninety-year-old batch of stolen coins ended up in the mud behind a small-town railroad museum.

CHAPTER SEVENTEEN

Chancy Conroy flipped the "open" sign over to "closed" and twisted the deadbolt lock on the front door, irritated. He had more important things to worry about than school kids sorting through boxes of pennies, hoping to find wheat backs. The day had been filled with bothersome customers, no one bringing him anything valuable or making a decent purchase. Sometimes he thought he'd just as soon sell off his inventory, close up shop altogether and retire – maybe to Miami or San Diego, somewhere with decent weather, an ocean view and nothing to do but refill a margarita before it ran dry.

His father had talked about doing just that, packing up and leaving. But Frank Conroy had been a man who persevered, yes indeed. Determined to find the coins, he lingered in Colorado for decades after the authorities cleared him of stealing those Double Eagles in 1926. Even on his deathbed, he couldn't give up the search. Chancy had been confused when his father held up two fingers and whispered, "Eagles." Thought the old man had lost the last bit of his sanity just before sliding out of this world. But the connection became clear as he sorted through his father's papers later on. Newspaper clippings about the investigation in the '20s told more of the story than Frank Conroy ever had. And a map of Colorado, marked up with locations and notes, had explained the many trips his father had taken over the years. He'd vanish for a few days and always return disgruntled.

Had his father, a Denver Mint guard at the time the coins went missing, actually been guilty of the theft? He'd probably never know. Frank Conroy had certainly never talked about it, and the newspaper articles only indicated he'd been accused and later cleared. On the one hand, if he'd taken the coins, why would he have had to search for them? Wouldn't he have known where they were? Perhaps he'd known the thief, but not the hiding place. Or maybe he *had* been guilty, but someone else hid the coins and double-crossed him in the end. It didn't matter. All Chancy cared about now was finding the coins. That's what his father had asked him to do in his last lucid moments.

Sitting down at his desk, he pulled the old map from a drawer and spread it out. The well-worn paper held almost a century of markings. His father had methodically covered areas close to Denver, but also farther away. Many circles and notes dotted locations around Colorado Springs and Alamosa. North of Denver, notes were scarce, indicating he'd focused on the southern half of the state. Additional towns to the south with heavy marks included Chama, New Mexico, and Durango.

It had taken Chancy some time to figure out the connection, but once he did, the method his father used for the hunt became clear. Each town with heavy markings had a train station. His father had been searching stops along the Denver & Rio Grande Railroad line.

It made sense to hide the coins at or near a train station. It would have been easy for the conspirators to pass the coins on to another person this way. It also made it convenient for the thief to retrieve the stash later as long as the hiding place was secure enough to prevent some outsider from stumbling on to their treasure. Inside a brick wall, perhaps?

Chancy sat back, folded the map, and returned it to the drawer. He'd been over it hundreds of times over the years, adding his own notes when he either retraced his father's steps or continued forward, focusing on the Durango area. That's where his father's notes had tapered down to almost nothing. The Durango-Silverton line was the one stretch that Frank hadn't explored.

Because there were so few stops between Durango and Silverton, it didn't take Chancy long to search the stations. Within a few months, he was convinced he'd inspected every brick, board and rail between the two towns. He decided to take a different approach: he'd let the coins come to him. He set up Chancy's Coin Shop in Silverton and slowly built steady business, hoping in time it would pay off, and what he'd been looking for all this time would come walking through the door.

Years passed with customers bringing him everything from a 1932-S Quarter to the elusive 1909-S Indian Head Cent, pieces that would make most coin shop owners happy. Even Double Eagles turned up sometimes, usually from years of low to medium value, but none from 1926. That is, until Paige MacKenzie showed up.

Now he was kicking himself. He'd allowed his excitement to show, and he'd been too aggressive about asking her where she found it. He'd been too eager. He could see it in her eyes, the recognition that the coin was special. Worse yet, he'd made a few calls after she and the man accompanying her left, trying to dig up more information. What he'd found out was worrisome. She was a reporter, which spelled "nosy" as far as he was concerned. Recklessly tipping her off that the coin could have a story behind it was stupid.

He'd also made a mistake when he offered to buy it so quickly, especially for that price. Five hundred dollars? He should have offered fifty, a less dramatic amount. She would have been less suspicious then, especially if he'd just made a casual comment. If she'd fallen for it, he would have saved several bucks, too.

He picked up the phone on his desk and dialed a number. As he waited for the other person to answer, he remembered the group of kids who'd made fun of his landline recently. He didn't really care. Plain old phones had served him well his entire life. Why would he want one of those new-fangled devices you could carry around in your pocket?

Tapping the eraser end of a pencil against his desk top, he waited for the call to connect. What was taking so long? How hard was it to pick up a phone and say "hello"? *Five rings, six rings, seven rings…*

"Hello?"

"What took you so long to answer," Chancy grumbled.

"Needed to get outside."

"Well, at least that was smart. Listen," Chancy continued. "We may have a problem. There's a reporter snooping around. I don't think she's on to anything in particular. But she came in asking about a coin. She had one with her, supposedly found it on the ground. Or someone did, I don't remember. But she had one, all right."

"A 1926 Double Eagle?"

"Yes," Chancy said. "In excellent shape, too. Close to mint condition."

"Sounds promising."

"I couldn't get any other information from her. She had a big guy with her."

"I'll find out more."

"I can't say where you'll find her. You'll just have to search around. She mentioned coming up from Durango."

"Don't worry. I know where she is."

"Then you should have called me first!" Chancy barked. "See what you can find out, and let me know."

He slammed the phone down and headed next door to cool off with a Butter Pecan Silver Scoop.

CHAPTER EIGHTEEN

"Horses?"

Paige took a sip of Chardonnay and leaned back, waiting for Jake to explain his plan. The cushioned booth and muted lighting at The Iron Horse comforted her after her afternoon of work. As much as she loved the Old West series she wrote for *The Manhattan Post*, she had to both weave and weed to pull the railroad article together. The western development of the railway system could fill several encyclopedia volumes. Still, she knew she'd find a good balance of history and general railroad nostalgia. Once she added a photo of an old steam engine, she'd end up with a reader-friendly piece. When Susan agreed via email, she'd closed her laptop with relief, knowing she was making good progress. She was ready to relax with her favorite cowboy.

"Yes, Paige, horses," Jake laughed. "I know you know what they are because you rode one when you were in Jackson Hole on your very first Old West assignment."

Paige reached across the table and gave Jake a playful slap, nearly knocking a basket of fresh sourdough bread over in the process.

"Of course I know what horses are. I just didn't know you were thinking about getting any, that's all."

"I grew up around horses," Jake said. "The Jackson property doesn't feel like a real ranch to me without them."

"Them...as in how many?" Paige swirled her wine around in her glass, placing silent bets on the answer.

"I think two, at least for now."

"To keep each other company?"

Jake smiled. "I suppose that's one reason. But it also means we can ride together when you come out."

The server placed two bowls in front of them and walked away.

"You're pretty self-confident, aren't you, Mr. Norris?" Paige resisted the temptation to reach across the table again, deciding two overturned bowls of corn chowder would be far worse than an off-kilter basket of bread.

"Confident enough," Jake said, dipping a piece of sourdough bread in the chowder and taking a bite. He closed his eyes and sighed, content. "Delicious."

Paige reached for a spoon and tried the soup. He was right; it was delicious.

"Why do I get the feeling you have other plans for these horses?"

Jake finished a second bite of combined soup and bread, and then switched to a spoon. "Because you're perceptive."

"Thank you," Paige said. "But it's not just that. I've watched you work to update the ranch. Slow and steady, as they say, without rushing."

"You're right," Jake said. "Part of that is because it needed work, and I wanted the renovations to be high quality. But I've also weighed ideas about what to do with the ranch. It's a large property. Too large for one person."

"Jake..."

"Wait." Jake stopped Paige before she could continue. "I'm not talking about you moving out there."

Oddly, Paige felt her stomach flip-flop. Although she hadn't committed to a move yet, she also hadn't ruled it out. As it was, her desire to move to Jackson Hole continued to grow. For that matter, each time they saw each other, the appeal tripled.

"What's that look on your face, Paige? You already know I'd love to have you out there with me. I'm talking about something bigger."

"Bigger than having me move to be with you?" Paige said, calmly, but firmly.

Jake sighed. "I'm kind of digging myself into a hole, huh?"

Paige couldn't hold back a giggle. "A little, but I'm teasing you. Go ahead. What plans?"

"I've been thinking – just thinking now, don't panic – about opening a guest ranch."

"A guest ranch?" Paige dropped her fork, which bounced to the edge of the table and landed in a side serving of au gratin potatoes, sticking out at an angle oddly resembling the Leaning Tower of Pisa. She hadn't even noticed the server switch the soup bowls for the main entrées. She'd been too engrossed in the conversation.

"I bet you couldn't do that again if you tried," Jake laughed.

"I'm sure you're right."

"Back to the topic. You think the guest ranch is a bad idea." Jake frowned.

"No, I think it's a great idea!"

"Really?" Jake looked half relieved, half shocked.

"Of course," Paige said. "You have a huge property that you're not yet using for anything. Jackson Hole gets swamped with visitors in the summer, plus another blast in the winter. It's tough to find lodging in the area during the main season. You're thinking of those cabins, aren't you? That's why you replaced the floorboards?"

"Yes and no," Jake said. "They had to be replaced, anyway. The wood was rotten from neglect. But, yes, I did have it in mind that someday I might want to use them for guests. And the farmhouse would make a perfect lodge."

"True," Paige said hesitantly. "But you live there."

"Then I wouldn't. It's simple. I can fix up one of the small cabins as a residence. Maybe add a room or two."

"And?"

Jake took a bite of pork tenderloin as Paige nibbled on a salad. Her work on the article, combined with the mystery of the coin, had stolen her appetite. Soup and salad seemed like the safest bet. Now she also had Jake's new plans to consider.

"And," he continued. "A fireplace, a partial fence for privacy, a back deck, some comfort additions like that."

"Sounds tempting, no question," Paige said. "What about the guest cabins? You only have a handful."

"That's enough to start. Better to begin small, anyway. Smooth out all the details and possible problems before expanding. I can build more later if I need to."

"I agree with that," Paige said. "I've watched businesses expand too quickly. It's not always pretty. My uncle opened a pizza shop in New York, an extremely popular business there, of course. But he took short cuts and didn't do enough research on his competition. He was too stubborn to bother with a feasibility study. He had to close within the year."

Jake shook his head. "I'm sorry to hear that. I've watched people open businesses before, too. Some taking it slow, some rushing ahead. The advance legwork is crucial."

"When are you thinking to open it?"

"Not until late next spring. Summer's already winding down, and I have plenty of planning and research to do, not to mention acquiring remodeling permits and all that. I'm thinking of this as a seasonal business – late spring to early fall, since I won't be involved in the winter's ski season. A lot of guest ranches focus on a single season. Plus, I need time to get it ready, and construction is next to impossible in the winter, as you know."

Paige finished her salad. Jake still worked on the last few bites of his larger meal.

"So you'd wait to get the horses? This is part of your advance planning?"

"Actually, no." Jake now pushed his plate aside, next to Paige's. "We'd need more for the guest ranch, especially if we wanted to offer horseback riding. But I'd like a couple now."

"So you'll look for some when you get back?" Paige accepted a cup of coffee and watched the server fill a cup for Jake, as well.

"Probably," Jake said. "But I did have an interesting talk with Stephen Porter today while you were returning the coin to Sam. He said his friend in Durango has a couple of beauties for sale."

"What kind?" It seemed the right question to ask, though Paige knew very little about horses.

Jake leaned forward over his coffee, encouraged by Paige's interest. "One's a quarter horse, good temperament and used to riders. The other is an appaloosa."

"Oh, I've seen pictures of them," Paige said. "They're beautiful."

"Yes, they are. And this one is calm; at least that's what Stephen said. He's ridden her before."

"They sound like good choices."

"They have one more, an Arabian. I'm not sure she's right for my ranch."

"Why not?"

"She's young and hot. Could be trouble down the line."

Paige paused. Just hearing the words *she's young and hot* coming out of Jake's mouth gave her a start.

"Paige," Jake said, laughing. "We're talking about horses, remember? By young, I mean green broke. She's just learned to saddle up. I wouldn't put an inexperienced rider on her. I could probably handle her, but she'll still need more training."

"And what about her being 'hot'?" Paige asked, trying to keep a straight face.

"That's more of a temperament description. A hot horse can be unpredictable, another reason the horse should have an experienced rider."

They finished their coffee, paid the check and walked back to the inn. They'd skipped dessert, but the cool night air felt like the perfect finale to the enjoyable meal. Jake wrapped his arm around Paige and pulled her close. She leaned her head against his shoulder, and they fell into an awkward gait, but neither of them was willing to separate.

"How sure are you?" Paige asked.

Jake remained quiet, as if mulling over her question.

"About the guest ranch," Paige added quickly.

"I'd say eighty percent."

"Really? I have a feeling you'll do it then."

"I think so," Jake said. "But I'm not rushing into it. I'll draw up a business plan and make sure it's feasible. But the horses are another story. I'd like to get two, whether or not the guest ranch is a go."

Paige straightened up, a possible outing taking shape.

"You said those horses were in Durango, right?"

"That's right," Jake said. "But if you think we can ride the train down and bring them back with us, there'll be some logistical problems."

"Funny." Paige punched him jokingly in the shoulder. "No, I was just thinking you might want to go see them, maybe tomorrow, or at least call and talk to the owner."

"I wouldn't mind that," Jake agreed. "Good suggestion. What brings this on?

"What do you mean?" Paige attempted to sound innocent, but knew she fell short.

"Because there's always a reason behind your sudden impulses, whether it's a question or a trip. I appreciate that you'd like me to follow up on the horses, but what else are you after in Durango?"

"Possible information."

"Care to elaborate?"

"Sure." Paige paused, figuring out the best explanation. "I was talking to Jesse earlier, at the museum."

"Right. You said returning the coin to Sam went well."

"Yes, it did," Paige said. "She had no idea it wasn't the original. I was relieved. I'm not sure how I would have explained the need to leave the other one there."

"You could have just told her it was so special they wanted to inspect it longer," Jake said.

"That might have worked," Paige agreed. "Fortunately, I didn't have to try. After I finished with Sam, I had an interesting conversation with Jesse, and he dropped a tidbit of Hutchins family history into my hands that may be useful."

They reached the steps of the inn, but settled on the front porch to talk privately. Paige lowered her voice.

"Jesse's grandmother is still alive. She's in an assisted living facility in Durango."

"I'm not sure I get the connection."

"The connection is that she's Jasper's widow."

"Which one is Jasper again? This family didn't make it easy to remember their names."

"Jasper is the one who worked at The Denver Mint at the time the coins went missing. At least that's when I think he was there."

"And you think she'll know something about the coins?"

"Maybe," Paige said. "Jesse said she isn't always coherent. She tells lots of stories, but I suspect fact is mixed with fantasy. The nurses call her 'The Bird Lady.' Sort of an odd coincidence, don't you think? Sam calls her coin a bird. Pearl might know something about the coins."

"How old is she? Those coins were stolen in 1926. Maybe you have the generations wrong. She must be Jesse's great-grandmother."

Paige shook her head adamantly. "No, I don't. Jasper married her in 1932. She was his second wife, only eighteen at the time. He was ten years older than she was. She's one hundred one now."

Jake whistled. "I bet she *does* have tales to tell."

"Yes, according to Jesse, she loves to tell stories. The only problem is figuring out which ones are real and which ones she made up."

"And the bottom line is that you want to go see her."

"How did you know?" Paige smiled, barely visible in the evening porch light.

Jake laughed. "Just a wild guess. But I'm up for it. Two horses and one elderly woman? What better reason could there be for a road trip? Or, rail trip, as it may be."

"Great." Paige leaned over to hug Jake, who immediately pulled her into his lap.

"Maybe we should take this discussion inside," Jake said as he ran his hand through her hair and softly kissed her. Paige took a few seconds to catch her breath.

"I think that's a perfect idea."

CHAPTER NINETEEN

Paige stepped off the train in Durango, Jake just behind her. A short walk from the station put them on Main Avenue not far from the historic Strater Hotel.

"Impressive," Jake said, noting the four-story, red brick structure.

"Yes," Paige agreed. "I stopped in there to browse while I waited for the train to Hutchins Creek the other day. The Denver & Rio Grande Railroad founded Durango in 1881 after building the San Juan Extension. The Durango-Silverton line opened in 1882. A growing town needs a hotel, and the Strater opened in 1887. Plus the railroad management knew they could promote the line between Durango and Silverton as a scenic passenger route right from the start. Of course, it's also been used to transport hundreds of millions of dollars of precious metals for the mining industry over the years."

"Well, they sure did a good job on this hotel."

"No question. And they keep it up, too. It has the largest antique walnut furniture collection in the world. Great saloon, too – the Diamond Belle."

"And you're familiar with the saloon...how?"

Paige laughed. "I should make up a wild story to get back at you for asking me that, but the truth is, I was thirsty and needed easy access to iced tea."

"OK, I'll buy that. So where to now?"

"Hopefully to get more information about the coin."

"Lead the way."

Another quarter mile stroll along Main Avenue, followed by three blocks up a side street, brought them to the Mountain Serenade Home of the Rockies.

"This is the place," Paige said, double checking printed notes she pulled from her jeans pocket. "Room 124, so Jesse told me." She folded the paper and slipped it back in her pocket. "Let's go."

Inside, the building was tidy and clean, yet seemed friendly. Bright rays of sunshine filtered down from skylights in the atrium. A bulletin board displayed colorful posters, photos and activity schedules. A nurses' station off to one side gave off a professional vibe without seeming cold or unapproachable. Those on duty appeared to be in good spirits. One looked up immediately to say hello.

Paige stepped forward and introduced herself and Jake.

"We're here to see Pearl Hutchins," Paige said, suddenly hoping she wouldn't be turned away as a non-relative. Why hadn't that crossed her mind before?

"How nice," the woman's name tag read "Ellie," and she appeared to be old enough to be a resident herself. "You came just at the right time. Pearl's in the activity room right now." Ellie raised her arm and pointed to a large room just off the atrium. A dozen residents filled the room, playing cards or board games, or entertaining visitors. "Just sign in on this clipboard – names, person you're visiting, date and time – and go right in. She's the woman in a blue dress over by the checkers table."

Paige breathed a sigh of relief as she filled out the form and handed the pen to Jake. She thanked Ellie. As she moved toward the activity room, she heard a light fluttering sound.

"Look." Paige motioned to Jake quickly, pointing to the source of the noise. Four bird cages sat around the room, in corners or against walls, each with two feathery inhabitants busy chirping to neighbors or picking at birdseed. Her hopes plummeted.

"Now, that's a great idea," Jake said, oblivious to Paige's disappointment. "Makes this place feel like more of a home.

It's a nice touch." He caught the look on Paige's face and paused. "What's the matter? Don't you think so?"

Paige folded her arms. "Of course I do, Jake. But don't you see? *These* must be the birds Pearl talks about. Why didn't it occur to me? Naturally they'd have birds, or fish, or some sort of low maintenance pets for the residents."

"That never occurred to me, either," Jake said. "You might be right."

"What did you just say?" Paige fought to keep a straight face.

"I said you might be…hey, that's not funny."

"I wouldn't mind getting that statement on tape," Paige laughed.

"So you can use it against me in the future? Not a chance."

Paige moved to one of the bird cages, then on to the others. Parakeets with brilliant blue and green feathers filled the first two enclosures. Another held white and gray doves, while the fourth displayed canaries – one a bright orange, the other a combination of orange and brown. The cages were large with natural branches, fresh water and toys, their inhabitants delighted to glide across the generous spaces from one perch to another.

"They're beautiful," Paige remarked. "Free, light-hearted. When I was growing up, we didn't have pets. What about you?" She peered at one of the canaries and attempted a light whistle. The bird cocked its head to the side and stared without responding.

"Horses and dogs," Jake said. "A barn cat or two along the way. We had some hawks around the property, but nothing delicate like these."

Watching Jake observe the birds brought a sudden swell of joy to Paige's heart. His rugged looks and tall, lean stature next to the tiny creatures created an oddly complementary contrast. He fit in anywhere. And he fit into her life perfectly; she couldn't deny it.

"Here," Paige said, motioning toward the checkers table. "Let's talk to Pearl." She grabbed Jake's hand and tugged once, then headed across the room.

Pearl Hutchins was a frail woman, both physically and in countenance. She sat in a wheelchair, pulled up to a game table, but didn't touch the checkers in front of her. Her eyes were closed, and her head swayed lightly, presumably in time to a medley of songs from the '40s that flowed from the room's speakers. As Paige and Jake approached, she opened her eyes.

"Hello, Pearl," Paige said, bending forward to greet the woman. She placed a hand softly on Pearl's shoulder and pulled out a chair with the other to sit beside her. Jake took a seat also, letting Paige do the talking.

"We're staying in Hutchins Creek, at the inn with Rose," Paige explained. "Rose and Jesse suggested you might like visitors, so we came down on the train to say hello."

"The Morning Star," Pearl whispered.

"Yes, well, no," Paige said. "We didn't ride The Morning Star, but we've seen it."

A huge grin spread across the old woman's face, as if the mere mention of the train car had brought sun to the afternoon. And perhaps it had, Paige thought. Memories could do that.

"Jasper loves that car."

"I can see why," Paige said, smiling across the table at Jake. The use of present tense in speaking of her late husband was poignant and sweet. "It's a beautiful car."

"So beautiful." Pearl reached forward with a trembling hand and moved a red checker from one square to another. She paused and moved it back, her expression uncertain.

In a gesture that brought another wave of joy to Paige, Jake leaned closer to the table and slid a black checker forward one space, then sat back. Paige watched as Pearl made eye contact with Jake, and then lowered her eyes to regard the board. She made no move, but looked content.

"You have a wonderful family, Pearl," Paige ventured. "Rose and Jesse have been excellent hosts while we've been visiting. And you have a lovely home here, too. I especially love the birds."

"So many birds," Pearl said. "So many."

Paige nodded. "I especially love the green parakeets. Which ones are your favorites?"

"They're all so shiny!" Pearl looked delighted as she continued her description. "Jasper takes good care of them, you know."

"I'm sure he does," Paige said, thinking. "How many birds does he take care of?"

"So many birds. So many shiny birds."

Paige sighed as she smiled and took the woman's hand. "I'm sure he takes good care of them all."

"Not anymore," Pearl said, a frown creasing her brow. "Roosevelt has them."

Paige and Jake exchanged looks and spoke at the same time. "Roosevelt?"

Another resident approached the table, sat and moved a checkers piece. Instead of answering their question, Pearl moved her own piece.

"Joe," Ellie appeared and leaned forward. "Pearl has company right now. Maybe you'd like to play cards with Millie? She was asking about you at breakfast."

"Don't worry," Paige said, standing up. "We just stopped by to say hello, anyway. And Pearl looks like she's ready to take on the checkers challenge."

"I always win," Pearl announced, grinning at Joe, who grinned back.

"That's true," Ellie said. "But today might be Joe's day to win." Ellie winked at Paige.

"I think it'll be a tough contest," Jake said, also standing.

"I agree." Paige said a quick farewell to Pearl and thanked Ellie. Leaving Pearl and Joe to battle out the game, she and Jake headed for the exit. She stopped once briefly at each bird cage for another look, then headed out.

* * *

Jake stuck his cell phone in his pocket, sat down and took a gulp of coffee. He looked around at the activity inside the Diamond Belle Saloon. "No luck reaching the owners of those horses. It was a long shot, anyway, without an appointment. I'll call again tomorrow. How long until Henry meets us?"

"Not long," Paige said, glancing at her cell phone. "He was just picking up supplies for Rose that would be ready at 5 p.m. Then he said he'd swing by and give us a ride back to the inn."

"Convenient that he had errands in Durango today," Jake said. "Not that I would have minded a night here, if only to listen to that ragtime piano. I bet this place gets hopping later on at night. We could have had a night out and taken the train back up to Hutchins Creek in the morning."

"A northbound afternoon train would have been even more convenient," Paige pointed out. "But that's not how the schedule works. I'm glad we mentioned we were coming down here to Henry. I don't mind a ride back, even if I have to dodge that glove compartment a dozen times."

"I don't mind doing the dodging," Jake offered. "Lulu's no match for me. You sit where you're safe, and I'll fight the good fight."

Paige laughed as she picked up a tabletop menu and looked it over. "Are you sure coffee's enough for you? The potato skins on the Happy Hour menu look tempting."

"Not as tempting as a steak and baked potato with all the fixin's at The Iron Horse. I don't want to ruin my appetite."

"I doubt that's possible," Paige laughed. She'd never seen Jake have trouble finishing a meal. Because of his work outdoors, he always built up a good appetite. "I heard Rose is cooking something up at the inn."

"Well, then, that's another reason to stay hungry." Jake took another gulp of coffee and leaned back in his chair. "So what do you make of the visit to Pearl?"

Paige pondered her iced tea before speaking up. "I'm not sure. When I first saw the bird cages, I thought Jesse's comment about Pearl talking about birds referred to the parakeets and doves, that it had nothing to do with the coins. But when I asked her which color her favorites were, she said 'shiny.' I took a second look at the birds on the way out, to see if any had shimmery wings, or something that would match her description. They didn't. So I think she had to be talking about the coins."

"If there *are* any other coins, Paige," Jake pointed out. "We don't know that for sure. It could be a fluke that Sam found one. Not to mention the possibility that the coin might not even be from the stolen batch."

"Well, someone *did* steal the coins even if they weren't ever in Hutchins Creek," Paige insisted. "You heard what the detectives at the Denver Mint said. I believe the coin Sam found is from that stolen batch. Why else did Chancy get so intense and weird when he saw it? He must know about the coins, too. Don't forget his father worked at the Mint when the coins went missing."

"But he was cleared," Jake pointed out.

"That doesn't mean he wasn't guilty. Only that he got away with it."

"We still don't know for sure that Frank was Chancy's father. Conroy is a common name. It could just be coincidence," Jake said.

"Well, I'm certain Frank is his father." Paige said. "I did a little online research."

Jake laughed and patted his mouth with his napkin. "You *stalked* him."

"I *researched* him. It's not the same thing at all."

"Back up a minute," Jake said. "What was the deal about Roosevelt? Pearl lost me there. I figured she was just confused."

Paige sighed. "I can explain that, I think. Remember Chancy explained that Roosevelt recalled gold in 1933?"

"Right." Jake nodded. "So maybe Jasper did have coins, or Chancy's father had them..."

"Or both..." Paige offered.

"But then they were turned in when Roosevelt mandated it," Jake said. "Which would mean they aren't around anymore."

"Don't forget, they were allowed to keep one hundred dollars' worth. That would have been five coins. So if Sam found one, there could be four others. But..." Paige's voice faded away as thoughts ran through her head.

"But, what?"

"But why would anyone risk turning in stolen coins?"

"Good point," Jake admitted. "Yet Pearl thinks 'Roosevelt has them.'"

"That makes sense to me," Paige said. "If she knew about the coins – which I think she did, based on her comment about them being shiny – she would have expected Jasper to turn them in. But if they were stolen, Jasper couldn't have turned them in. He might have told Pearl he handed them over to the government, but maybe he didn't actually do it."

"You're saying if he *had* the coins, he must have hidden them." Jake paused as a server refilled his mug.

"Exactly," Paige said.

"Maybe Jasper had nothing to do with it. Maybe Chancy's father, the guard, had the coins and hid them."

"Then why would one coin end up behind the Hutchins Creek Railroad Museum?" Paige asked.

"Maybe Chancy's father hid them in Hutchins Creek to make Jasper look guilty if someone found the coins. Or it could be that Jasper and Frank Conroy were working together and decided to stash them on the museum grounds."

"Possible," Paige said. "But remember it wasn't a museum back then. It was the original train station. The museum was established later, when the new train depot went in."

Jake pointed toward the front window, where Henry was pulling up to the curb in his faithful sidekick, Lulu. "Too many possibilities," he said.

"Yes, but only one is accurate." Paige stood up to gather her things for the ride back. "We just have to figure out which one."

CHAPTER TWENTY

Paige reached for a breadbasket and pulled out a fresh square of cornbread. Dinner at the inn with Rose's cooking beat out Jake's suggestion to eat at The Iron Horse, and he showed no regret as he dug in to his meal. Paige thought the spread resembled a holiday feast. Jake's plate featured edge-to-edge portions of ribs, scalloped potatoes, green bean casserole and cornbread. Similar plates sat before Jesse, Henry, Stephen and Rose. Paige, Sam and Tommy's servings were smaller, yet still generous.

"How was your visit to Pearl today," Jesse asked as he reached for a tub of honey butter for his bread.

"Fine," Paige said. "She seems like a sweet lady."

"She's very sweet," Rose agreed. "Always treated us well when we were growing up. Don't you think so, Jesse?"

"Absolutely. Dad used to get upset with her, told her she was spoiling us."

Paige laughed. "That's what grandparents are for, right?"

"That's the way I see it," Rose said, smiling. "The same goes for aunts. That's how it should be, right, Samantha?"

"Right," Sam chirped. She blew into her straw, and the milk in her glass bubbled up. Jesse tapped her arm and she stopped. Tommy mimicked Sam and earned his own tap from his father.

"Did she tell you any good stories today?" Henry asked. Jesse gave him a look that struck Paige as peculiar.

"We just talked casually," Paige said, sending a similar look to Jake, a cue for him to not dive into specifics. "She was playing checkers in the game room."

"That's her table," Rose said. "She does like shoving those checkers around."

"I'll agree with that." Stephen spoke up for the first time. "I've never seen her sit anywhere else."

"How nice," Paige remarked. "You've visited her?"

"Sure," Stephen said. "We live right down the street. It's easy to stop by now and then. I didn't visit my grandmother often enough after she moved into an assisted living facility; I was too young to know better and too busy trying to make ends meet. Pearl reminds me a little bit of her, eases my sadness at Gran's passing."

Paige appreciated the sentiment, but wondered if Stephen's reasons for visiting Pearl were a little more complicated than he was saying. He seemed more involved with the Hutchins family than a typical inn guest. Then again, he stayed with Rose frequently, and he'd admitted that the inn felt like home. It made sense that he'd grown close to Rose, Jesse and other residents of Hutchins Creek.

"How long have you been coming here?" Paige asked.

"Oh, gosh, years now. Ten, twelve?"

"I'd say more like fifteen," Henry said.

"I'm not fifteen yet," Tommy added.

"You will be one day, son," Stephen said. "No use rushing."

"Fifteen years sounds about right," Rose said. "Dad was still alive when you first started staying here."

"That's right," Stephen said. "Jerome was a fine man. He put up with my arrogance when I was young. I was honored to know him."

"He did always love your visits," Rose said, looking first at Stephen and then at Henry. "I remember all three of you sitting on the front porch and talking for hours."

"That we did," Stephen said, nodding his head.

"He thought of both you and Henry as family," Rose said, "just as I do."

Rose stood and retreated to the kitchen, returning with a full breadbasket. "More cornbread, anyone?"

"I don't think I could possibly eat more," Jake said. "This is fantastic. I've already had seconds on the potatoes."

"Well, save some room for pecan pie," Rose said. "I baked one this morning."

"Oh dear," Paige said. "I'm going to gain five pounds while I'm here. I'd better go twice as far on my run tomorrow morning."

"I don't force anyone to eat," Rose laughed.

"Of course not," Henry piped up. "You don't have to."

A phone rang in the kitchen, and Rose scurried back to answer it. She returned after just a few minutes.

"That was fast for a reservation," Jesse said.

"No reservation," Rose explained. "Actually it was the Mountain Serenade Home."

All conversation stopped as everyone at the table seemed to feel a flutter of apprehension.

"Oh, no, don't worry," Rose said quickly. "Pearl is fine. They just wanted to leave a message for Paige. They found a Hutchins Creek Railroad Museum sweatshirt and thought it might be hers."

"Mine?" Paige asked. "No, I don't have a museum sweatshirt." She turned to Jake. "You don't either, do you?"

"No," Jake said, shaking his head, "though I've wanted to pick a couple up."

"Discounts for guests of the inn," Jesse said.

"Well, it must have belonged to someone who was visiting another resident," Rose said. "Plenty of people have those sweatshirts. We've been selling them for years."

"Was it blue? I might have left a blue one there last time I visited. I tried to find it the other day and couldn't. Had to wear red." Jesse helped himself to another piece of cornbread.

"Not blue. The woman who called said it was brown, so I didn't think it would belong to Paige or Jake," Rose said.

"I like red," Tommy said, his face lighting up. "Fire trucks are red. I got to ride in a fire truck once."

"Really?" Paige said. "You are so lucky. I've never been in a fire truck." She glanced at Jake, who winked at her.

"It was really cool!" Tommy said. "I got to wear a hat, too, but it was too big for me. I'm going to be a fireman when I grow up, though. The hat will fit me then because I'll be big."

Paige smiled. "That sounds like a good plan." She turned toward Rose. "So you said the sweatshirt was brown? I don't think I noticed any brown sweatshirts in the museum gift shop."

"We only carry blue and red now," Jesse said. "They match our engineer outfits. Plus, customers prefer blue and red. Whoever left that sweatshirt at the home must have bought it years ago. Awful things Dad stocked when he ran the museum: brown with green lettering. Those were some ugly sweatshirts."

"Jesse," Rose said. "Dad meant well. He just didn't have...fashion sense."

A ripple of laughter around the table followed Rose's comment.

"Isn't that the truth," Jesse laughed. "He was a good man, loved that museum. We had to mark those sweatshirts down so low we practically gave them away. In fact, I think we *did* give them away; we donated them to a thrift shop when the new ones came in."

Rose stood and began to clear the table, turning down offers of help. Whisking the dinner dishes into the kitchen, she returned with dessert plates and forks, followed by pecan pie. Jake and Jesse accepted slices, Paige turned the pie down, and Tommy asked for two pieces, triggering more laughter. After a round of coffee and words of thanks to Rose, Henry left to walk with Stephen. Tommy and Sam headed to the front parlor to play a board game. Jesse insisted that since he was Rose's actual family, she should let him help clean up. Paige and Jake took their coffee out to the gazebo.

"What a long day," Paige said, settling comfortably into Jake's arms, hands wrapped around the mug of French roast. She drew the coffee in close to her chest, feeling its warmth mix with that of Jake's embrace. A crescent moon looked down through branches of quaking aspen, and a light breeze flowed through the leaves. It was as if the world were rustling.

"An excellent day," Jake replied. He held his own coffee in his free hand and rubbed Paige's shoulder with the other. His fingers trailed upward to her neck and lightly brushed her earlobe. Paige shivered at his touch.

"Are you cold?"

Paige smiled and buried her head against Jake's chest. "You know I'm not."

"Ah," Jake teased. "You admit I have an effect on you. What caused that sweet reaction? Was it this?" He traced his fingers along her neck again.

"I suppose…" Paige said, trying to sound indifferent, though she heard her voice waiver.

"Or maybe it's something more like this." Jake set his coffee down on the small gazebo table and leaned closer to Paige, his lips softly caressing the side of her neck.

"Maybe…something…like…that…" Paige whispered.

"Or how's this?"

Jake lifted Paige's coffee mug from her hands and placed it on the table, next to his. Cupping her face with both hands, he kissed each eyelid and then let his lips travel to her mouth. Paige melted into the passion as his kiss deepened. He slipped his arms down her back and under her T-shirt, his determined hands flowing over her bare skin. Paige marveled at his touch – so strong, yet so gentle.

At the sound of hushed voices, Paige and Jake detached from each other and tried to regain their composure. Since dark was falling quickly now, the couple couldn't quite see who approached, though it was most likely Stephen and

Henry returning from their walk. But the discussion did not sound friendly.

Paige touched Jake's arm, a silent plea for him to remain quiet. She leaned forward, attempting to hear even part of the conversation, but the voices were too muffled. Soon the two figures disappeared along the side of the inn.

"What do you make of that?" Paige whispered.

"Beats me. You're the resident eavesdropping expert," Jake said. He squeezed Paige's hand so she'd know he was teasing. "My guess would be Stephen and Henry."

"That's my guess, too, but why would they be arguing? They seemed fine at dinner."

"Maybe they disagreed about favorite sports teams, or they might have gotten into a political discussion during their walk. That'll do it for a lot of people."

Paige shook her head. "No, it's something more."

They heard a door close. Paige waited to see if the two figures would reappear. Instead, just one figure walked back to the street and turned down the block. An engine fired up shortly afterwards, and soon a car passed by, turned a corner and drove away. From the gazebo, Paige couldn't see the car very well. But she saw it well enough to know it was tan.

CHAPTER TWENTY-ONE

Paige picked up a sweet potato fry and waved it in the air as she spoke. To other diners at the Rail Café, she might have looked like she was conducting a lunch symphony. For Paige, the discussion was serious. For Jake, it provided a perfect opportunity to joke.

"So, two men walked into a bar…"

"Jake, be serious."

"*You* be serious," he laughed. "You're the one waving a French fry around."

Paige put the fry down and leaned forward, lowering her voice. "Two men walked out of the house. Two men walked back in. Then only one walked out."

"You have to admit that sounds like a riddle."

"Jake," Paige warned.

"Right," Jake said. "That's what I saw, too."

"Stephen and Henry are the two who walked out, after dinner."

"Yes, at least they're the two who *said* they were going out." Jake lifted his bottle of beer, took a drink, and set the bottle back on the table. He wrapped his hands around his Boxcar Burger and took a bite. Paige had to give him credit for being patient. She'd talked through the scenario half a dozen times already.

"Then it would seem logical that Stephen and Henry were the two who walked back in."

"Agreed," Jake said between bites.

"But only one came back out, and I'm telling you it had to be Chancy Conroy."

"Because of the car that drove away," Jake said. "But you can't be sure it was his car. It was almost dark and the street lights aren't that bright. Maybe you saw Lulu."

"Wrong shape and color. Just stay with me here," Paige said. "Let's assume for a minute it *was* Chancy. That means one of the men who walked out didn't come back."

Jake nodded. "Or only one walked out originally. They both said they were going out walking, but we didn't actually watch them walk away. Maybe one decided not to go."

"But which one?" Paige's exasperated tone underscored her frustration.

"I have no idea," Jake said.

"And how did Chancy end up here, anyway?" Paige continued. "I'm telling you, he's after the coins. You saw his reaction to that single coin. I'll bet he thinks the rest are here somewhere, and he's working with one of the other guys to find them."

"That means you think he's connected somehow to either Henry or Stephen."

"Maybe," Paige said. "Or he's trying to get information from them. Or access to the museum, or something like that. Whoever just met with Chancy might not even know what he's after. He struck me as the sneaky type right from the beginning."

"I agree with you about that," Jake said. "I disliked the guy immediately. But the person we just saw leave the inn may *not* be Chancy."

Paige ignored this, took a sip of iced tea, and continued. "Rose is the one who recommended we go see Chancy originally. Stephen was there and overheard that. Maybe he already knew Chancy. He could have been with him last night."

"Maybe," Jake said. "Or that could be coincidence. If Chancy thinks you can lead him to the coins, he's going to look for you, and Hutchins Creek is a logical place for you to be. He might just be after information. Maybe he bumped into Stephen and Henry by chance. It could be that one of the guys came back early, and we didn't notice, since we were…"

"Otherwise occupied?" Paige smiled, remembering the affectionate moments in the gazebo the night before. Anyone could have walked past without them noticing.

"Exactly."

"One way or another, there's an intricate connection between some of these people," Paige said.

"How do you figure that?"

Both paused as the server refilled Paige's iced tea and offered Jake another beer, which he declined. Paige thanked the server and turned back to Jake.

"Take Stephen and Chancy, for example. Rose suggested we go to Chancy to help us identify the coin. Stephen did seem interested in the coin. Maybe he's a coin collector. He might already know Chancy."

"OK, so you're saying they may know each other, even though Stephen didn't let on?" Jake said. "Sort of a long shot, Paige. You don't have any evidence of this."

"No, at least not yet," Paige agreed. "Then there's Henry and Chancy."

"Do they even know each other?" Jake asked. "Neither one has mentioned the other, unless you've heard something I haven't."

"Good point. But it doesn't mean they *don't* know each other. You know how it is in small towns and surrounding areas."

"True. I suppose anyone could know anyone."

"So that brings us back to Henry and Stephen." Paige paused. "Stephen is a regular guest at the inn, and Henry does a lot of shuttle service for Rose. I suspect he does other small tasks around the inn, too."

"Right. So they know each other, but probably just as acquaintances. Henry would know any regular visitors."

"Yes, but does he go for walks with other guests?" Jake took another bite of his burger and waited for Paige's response.

"Maybe, maybe not. But we still don't know they're the two who took that walk together last night. Maybe Jesse didn't stay to help Rose clean up. For all we know, Henry may have offered to stay after you and I headed for the gazebo, which means Jesse might have stepped out with Stephen instead. That could make sense. Stephen is a regular visitor and strong supporter of the museum. He and Tommy spend a lot of time there when he's in town. It stands to reason they'd be friends with Jesse."

Paige leaned back and sighed, switching the subject.

"It'll be nice when that train car gets fixed up," Paige said. "It's sad to see it in such terrible condition when the model inside looks so nice."

"It makes sense it would be in rough shape after all this time sitting there."

"Yes, but I've been thinking about a couple of the scratches. Now that I've seen them a few times, they look deliberate, as if someone purposely etched them with a rock."

"Sounds like something any troubled teen might do," Jake pointed out. "You're talking about graffiti?"

"Not really graffiti, at least not the kind we'd see in a city. More like this." Paige pulled a napkin from a stack on the table, took a pen out of her purse and drew three diagonal lines. She turned the sketch toward Jake and watched as he picked it up and studied it.

"Where did you find the marks? On what part of the car?"

Paige thought back to her most recent inspection of The Morning Star. "They're on the sides, very low. Why would that matter?"

"On both sides?"

"Yes, now that you mention it."

After Jake finished studying lines on the napkin, he set it down. "It's just a guess, but I'd say those are hobo codes."

"Hobo codes? What on earth does that mean?"

"It's something I learned from my uncle, the one who worked on the Transcontinental line. He told me about how the hobos who ride the rails use codes to communicate with and pass on information to each other. They mark signs, mailboxes, curbs or other landmarks to let others know if, for example, an occupant in a particular house is friendly and won't turn them away. Or they may mark places where travelers can find medical help. That sort of thing."

"Then what would this one mean?"

"If I'm not mistaken, a code with three diagonal lines indicates an unsafe area."

"So, on a train car, that would be a message to stay away from that car?"

"Seems right."

"That means someone felt The Morning Star was too dangerous to board."

Paige folded the napkin, stretched sideways and slipped it into her jeans pocket. "Let's go to the museum to talk to Jesse. He might know more about this."

Nodding, Jake finished his last bite and dropped enough bills on the table to cover the check and a tip. He followed Paige out the door.

* * *

When Paige and Jake arrived at the museum, it was empty of customers. Jesse was not at the front counter, though they could hear him on the phone in the back office. With the echoing acoustics of the empty building, his voice was clear; he was placing an order to restock model railroad supplies. Paige wandered to the back door and smiled when she saw Sam playing in the miniature train yard. The birdbath looked newly filled, and, from the gleam in the water, it appeared the replica coin was getting its daily cleaning.

"Nice to see you two," Jesse said as he emerged from the office, clad in his usual engineer's outfit. "Out enjoying the weather today?"

"Absolutely," Jake said, "along with a Boxcar Burger at the Rails Café."

"I hear you there," Jesse said. "That's my favorite item on their menu."

"Well, it doesn't match your sister's cooking, but that would be hard to do." Jake patted his stomach with a grin of satisfaction.

"No argument with that," Jesse agreed. "We all come running when Rose gets busy in the kitchen. She put on a fine feast last night."

"Are you men talking about food, by any chance?" Paige laughed as she walked from the back door to the counter. The boys nodded. "I can't blame you, not after that meal Rose served last night. I'm still full. I should have taken a walk after dinner, like you guys did."

"I wish I had, too," Jesse said, nodding. "I would have worked off more of the pecan pie if I'd walked than I did helping Rose with dishes. But I don't like leaving her with all the cleanup. She works hard enough running the inn."

"You're a good brother," Paige said lightly. She and Jake exchanged glances. Jesse had answered her hidden question.

"Oh, Jesse," Paige added casually, "I wanted to ask you a question that came up while I was doing research for my article." *Not entirely true*, Paige thought, *but not entirely a lie.* "I came across some references to hobos hopping trains. Do you ever see any of that activity around here?"

"No, not along this stretch of tracks. This line ends at Silverton, so there's no place for them to go from there. A hobo's aim is to travel," Jesse said. "Trains don't run into Durango, either, so this is an isolated line. And this line only runs passenger trains now. Hobos usually hop freight cars."

"Did they ever run freight trains through here? Or any other type of car?" Paige almost cringed at her weak attempt to pull more information from Jesse. She already knew the

Durango-Silverton line had been used to transport ore from the local area to smelters. But Jesse didn't necessarily know what she knew.

"Sure," Jesse said. "Coal cars, mainly. Someone could hop one of those. But that would have been years ago when the line still connected over to Alamonito. Those tracks are long gone. So, no, I haven't seen any train hopping here. Dad did, though, back when he worked the stretch from Alamonito to Durango."

"Your dad was Jerome, right?"

"Yep." Jesse nodded. "He used to tell us stories about scaring the hobos away. Can't say if they were true or not. He had a tendency to exaggerate, and he loved to spin a good tale. But he could be gruff and territorial, so I don't doubt he objected to freeloaders."

The front door opened, and Jesse called a friendly greeting to the small group of visitors who'd entered.

"I'm heading outside to say hello to Sam." Paige nodded toward the back door.

"I'll join you," Jake said, following Page out to the yard.

Sam waved to Paige and Jake as they approached. "Did you come to see my bird? It's taking a bath."

"I see that." Paige smiled.

Sam brushed dirt off her hands and reached into the water, holding up her prized possession.

"It looks nice and clean, Sam. Good job." Jake said as he leaned down, eye level with the coin. As usual, Paige noticed the smooth fit of his shirt and jeans over his body as he moved. Somehow he looked especially attractive while engaged in the relaxed conversation with the young girl. *I love how wonderful he is with children,* Paige thought.

Leaving Jake and Sam in an animated conversation about her "special treasure," Paige wandered over to The Morning Star. She spotted the three diagonal lines that she and Jake had discussed at lunch. Circling the car, she looked more closely at the matching mark on the back, scratched into the lower edge. The front and back etchings were unmistakably the same.

"Definitely hobo code." Jake surprised her since she hadn't heard him walk up behind her. She stood quickly and turned to face him, finding he'd backed her up suspiciously close to the side of the train car.

"What's that rule on personal space?" she teased. "Three feet away? Isn't that what they say?" She glanced around each of Jake's shoulders, confirming that no one was watching. "Or was that...three inches away?" Slyly, she grasped his shirt with both hands and pulled him closer.

"I think I'll go with the second rule," Jake said. "Though I think that's still a bit conservative." Playfully, he removed Paige's hands from his shirt and pressed against her, delivering a soft, yet passionate, kiss. Just as quickly, he stepped back grinning, nearly causing her to slide down the side of the train.

"Um... so, hobo code, you were saying..." Paige turned back toward the markings as she attempted to regain her breath. She leaned down to look at them again.

"Yes, I think someone put those marks there as a warning to stay away from the car," Jake said, inspecting the etched lines more carefully. "Maybe that's not a bad idea. It seems like you're falling into uncertain territory here."

"Uncertain territory seems to be a specialty of mine, particularly lately." Paige didn't dare look at Jake, knowing he was likely to catch the double meaning.

"Only uncertain if you want it that way," Jake said, running his fingers through her hair.

"Well," Paige said, standing up and shifting to a serious tone. "One thing is certain. I'd like to know why a warning was etched into The Morning Star."

"And you plan to find out, I suppose. Even if I try to talk you out of it." Jake said, sighing.

Again, Paige grasped Jake's shirt and pulled him close for a kiss, then moved her lips close to his ear just long enough to whisper, "Absolutely."

CHAPTER TWENTY-TWO

Rose greeted Paige and Jake as they entered the dining area in search of coffee. "You got a phone call while you were out." She handed Paige a note and retreated to the kitchen. The smell of cookies baking hovered in the air.

"Ferguson," Paige said, handing the paper to Jake. "I wonder what he wants. And why he didn't call my cell phone." She reached into her pocket, pulled her phone out, and sighed. "Of course, I turned it off when we went to lunch so I wouldn't disturb other customers." She rolled her eyes and pushed the power button on.

"And you forgot to turn it back on," Jake said.

"Exactly."

"Because you were distracted at the museum," Jake added.

"Yes, that's true."

"Especially in the back yard."

Paige crinkled her nose and pulled the phone message back.

"Oh, are there any new exhibits in the back yard?" Stephen asked from a corner chair, where he sat reading a railroad magazine. "I don't want to miss anything while I'm here."

Paige hadn't noticed anyone else in the room, and she was glad she'd only used the name "Ferguson" without adding "Detective" in front of it. She didn't feel like explaining their visit to the Denver Mint, and she'd begun feeling the less said, the better. Too many unresolved questions were floating around.

"Nothing new," Paige said. "Though Sam is having a lot of fun with the birdbath Henry built her."

"She loves that yard," Stephen said. "She's out there every time we come to visit. I think Tommy's a little sweet on her."

"Well, who can resist a pretty girl in a train yard, right?" Jake winked at Paige.

Paige left Jake to chat with Stephen while she took her coffee and the phone message outside. Settling into the gazebo for privacy, she listened to voicemail from the detective and then returned the call.

"Detective Ferguson here." The officer's voice was even and professional.

"Hello, Detective. Paige MacKenzie, returning your call." She doubted her voice sounded as calm as his. She was too eager to learn if Ferguson had more information about the coin.

"I just wanted to touch base with you about your visit the other day, to thank you for bringing in the coin and for letting us hold it temporarily."

"Of course," Paige said. "I'm thrilled we could help. That is, I don't know if we *did* help, but if the coin leads you to solving an old case, I'm glad. Did you find out anything new?" Paige knew she was pushing her luck. What the detectives did with the coin really wasn't her business. But she wasn't good at keeping her curiosity curbed.

"Nothing new," Detective Ferguson answered. "Except our lab says the coin is genuine, so it could be from the missing batch. Any chance you've found others like it since you got back to Hutchins Creek?"

"No," Paige said. "The little girl who found that one doesn't have any others."

"Well, I just wanted to check. With your journalism background, you seem like the type of person who'd scout around for information. If you find any other coins, could you give me a call? It could move our investigation forward."

Paige agreed, thanked him for the call, and promised to contact him if she found additional coins.

"That was a short call," Jake said, joining her as she was putting her phone away. "What did he want?"

Paige took a sip of coffee and pondered the answer. "Just to check in, apparently. He wondered if we'd found any other coins. I told him no."

"Mighty perceptive of him to know you'd be looking," Jake laughed. "You *are* looking, you know."

"Of course I'm looking," Paige laughed. "Who wouldn't be looking for a hidden cache of coins? You know I'm not the type to let a mystery pass by."

"No, you certainly aren't."

"But finding the coins doesn't interest me as much as finding out *if* they're here, *why* they're here, and *how* they got here." Paige took another sip of coffee and settled back in the chair. "I still think Chancy was hanging around here the other night. I'm sure it was his car. And he was arguing with someone. You heard that yourself."

"I heard angry voices, but can't say it was Chancy," Jake pointed out.

"I'm sure it was," Paige insisted. "But I don't know who would be arguing with him. That's what's driving me crazy. Was it Henry? Jesse? Stephen? Someone else?"

"So, what's your overall theory?" Jake sat back to listen. Paige felt a sudden, inexplicable urge to kiss him, so she did.

"Nice," Jake said, smiling. "What was that for?"

"For listening to me. For not making fun of my curiosity. For not *always* telling me to stay out of trouble."

"Just most of the time," Jake laughed.

"It's OK, I know I deserve it. You've gotten me out of tough spots a few times," Paige admitted. "But back to your question about my theory. I don't think Sam's coin is the only one around here. I think the other coins are hidden somewhere in Hutchins Creek, and Chancy is looking for them. I also think he's not the only one looking. He's either working with a partner, or someone is searching independently, and he's trying to stop them."

"Let's say all that is true. How did the coins get here?"

Paige lifted her coffee to her mouth, but lowered it without taking a sip. "We know that Chancy's father, Frank, was a guard at the Denver Mint when the coins went missing. Maybe Frank hid them here, but never told Chancy where."

Jake nodded. "OK, that's one possibility."

"Or someone else hid them here, and Chancy heard about it. You know how urban legends get passed around. Someone gets an inkling that there's a secret hoard of something somewhere, and people come out of the woodwork looking for it."

"For example, a cache of coins?"

"Exactly," Paige said.

Jake frowned. "Well, if someone hid them, and someone is looking for them, and someone is trying to keep them from being found…that spells danger to me. It may be time to back off this, Paige. Let the detectives from the Mint Police do their job."

"The coins would have been hidden a long time ago," Paige continued, ignoring Jake's words of caution. "Though…not necessarily. They may have been stashed in one location and then moved later."

"Which means they might not be here at all, even if they once were," Jake said. "Chancy might be on a wild goose chase."

"As well as anyone else looking for the coins," Paige added.

"That would include you," Jake said, smiling.

"But then what about the coin Sam found?" Paige paused, and then answered her own question. "Because they *were* here at some point, in the museum yard."

"Which was actually the train depot at the time the coins went missing."

"But the coins might not have been here back when the museum was the original depot," Paige added. "They could have been moved here later, or even recently. Or ... someone brought them through this area at one time and dropped one by accident. That would mean there aren't any coins here at all. It could be that simple."

"Nothing is ever that simple around you, Paige."

CHAPTER TWENTY-THREE

Paige stood just outside the railroad museum's back gate. A strong breeze had kicked up in the morning and now, early afternoon, it hadn't yet died down. Grateful she'd chosen jeans and a long-sleeved green sweatshirt instead of something lighter, she tightened the elastic band that held her hair back, securing it against the wind.

The yard looked lonely without Sam playing in her usual spots. But she wasn't surprised to find the back area empty. A sign on the front door of the museum had read, "Will return at 1:30." Paige assumed Jesse and Sam had taken a lunch break. Probably Lily had prepared something for them at the house, or they might have splurged for a meal at the Rails Café. Her bet was on lunch at the house, considering that Jesse was struggling to fund The Morning Star's restoration. She glanced toward the house, but knew they'd be eating indoors since the wind was too strong for lunch on the porch.

Opening the gate, she stepped inside and closed it behind her. The latch clattered as the gate fought against the wind. *It's a good thing all the exhibits are heavy,* Paige thought as she looked around the yard. Powerful as the wind was, it was no match for old train cars or bolted down accessories. Only the birdbath swayed.

Walking through the yard, Paige bypassed The Morning Star and moved on to look at other cars she hadn't yet inspected much. Several cars had been moved since the day before, though The Morning Star remained in its same, prominent place. It received the most attention, both because of the restoration project and because it rested near the back door. It sat on the branch of tracks connected to the main line, not far from a switch engine. Paige remembered Jesse explaining they used the engine to rearrange the exhibits sometimes.

The museum was fortunate to have the old train depot as a home. Bringing cars in to display had not been difficult, in view of the maze of tracks already in place. Although one line led off the property and connected to the main line from the current train station, different branches of tracks fanned out across the yard, each holding a different type of car – freight, flat, coal and—undoubtedly a favorite to visitors—a bright red cupola-style caboose.

As fond of a caboose as anyone, Paige started there. A sign detailed the history of the much-loved rear car on freight trains and explained its usage. Until the 1980s, the law required trains in the United States and Canada to have cabooses with a full crew. Crew members rode the caboose in order to easily handle switches, safeguard the end of the train and inspect for problems during stops. Depending on the length of a trip, the caboose might hold functional living quarters, cooking facilities and a cast iron stove. As time went on, technology advanced to the point that a caboose was no longer required.

Noting the absence of a rope chain, Paige climbed the stairs and looked around inside. While she hunted for potential hiding places for coins, she felt a twinge of sadness at the thought of technology replacing the caboose. Hadn't she stood by railroad tracks when she was a child waiting to see the caboose at the end of a passing train? A wave of nostalgia washed over her.

She tapped on walls, looked in drawers for false bottoms, jiggled the stairs below the cupola seating area, and inspected floorboards, but found nothing intriguing. Discouraged, she stood up and sighed. It was pointless. If coins had been hidden in as simple a place as behind a board, surely someone would have found them long ago.

Moving on, she inspected the other cars in the yard. Each had served a specific purpose: carrying silver and gold ore, transporting coal, or bringing supplies to miners in the area. The importance of the railway system to modern day commerce was not only evident, but also remarkable.

Circling back to The Morning Star, she reflected on its appeal to visitors. The shiny model in the museum certainly added to its interest, but she suspected another draw. As the only passenger car on the lot, it represented the adventure of travel, as if the seats inside were calling "all aboard," to those outside.

Paige approached the car and lightly touched the side, feeling the curls of peeling paint. Recalling Jesse's comments about money going missing, she wondered why anyone would not want the car restored. Jerome had wanted it left as is, but he was gone, and Jesse had made it clear that the museum's goal was to return it to its original state. Rose seemed to support all the museum's projects. So did Henry. It didn't make sense. It seemed more likely that the missing money was simply that: missing money, unrelated to the restoration efforts.

Paige heard a screen door slam in the distance, and she looked up and waved at Jesse and Sam as they walked from the house to the yard. She joined them as they entered and reopened the museum.

"I had a peanut butter sandwich for lunch," Sam announced. Her wide smile indicated this to be a favorite food.

"Sounds delicious," Paige said. "Did your dad have the same thing?"

Sam shook her head. "He doesn't like peanut butter. Lily fixed him tuna with pickles. He likes pickles." She hopped back and forth from one foot to the other, a two-footed pogo stick. "And we both had potato chips. I always share my chips," she added, her expression serious.

Paige smiled. "I believe in sharing, too, Sam. Good for you."

"Yep," Sam chirped, proudly skipping off to explore the back yard again. Henry walked through the front door just as Sam skipped out the back. He sported his trademark tan fisherman's hat and bolo tie, this time with overalls and a blue flannel shirt with frayed cuffs and a tear in one sleeve.

"Saw this on your porch," Henry said as he placed a small package on the counter.

Jesse glanced at the address label and nodded. "Finally. About time that order of train whistles arrived." He opened the box and filled a counter top display, pulling it slightly back from the edge. Paige could imagine the potential commotion of having the whistles in the reach of young children

"So what are you up to today, Henry?"

"Nothin' much," Henry said. "Just working on Lulu. She could use some new spark plugs. I aim to pick some up and put them in tomorrow."

"Why not have the guys do it for you down at the garage? Save yourself the trouble." Jesse glanced at Paige and smiled, obviously knowing Henry would veto his suggestion.

"Rather do it myself," Henry huffed. "In my day, we did things ourselves."

"OK, Henry," Jesse laughed, "You do it your way." Turning toward Paige, he placed a flat hand to one side of his mouth and whispered, "Stubborn."

"I heard that," Henry quipped.

"Of course," Jesse laughed. "I meant for you to hear it. You'd be smart to embrace modern times now and then."

"Don't bet your money on that, Jesse. I ain't fixin' to do it anytime soon." With that, Henry lifted one hand in a hint of a wave, and left.

Paige returned the wave as the front door closed behind Henry, and then turned back to Jesse, who had moved a batch of papers to the front counter to sort.

"I've got to get these invoices in order." Jesse picked one out from the middle of the stack and put it on top. "Try to get a few of them paid this week. We've had some shortages in the register lately. I still don't understand it. It's not much, but it adds up."

Paige simply nodded. Jesse had no reason to know she was already aware of the missing money since she overheard this information when she was standing outside the window. "That's a problem many businesses face. Do you have any employees you don't know well? Anyone you hired recently, perhaps?"

"Not a one. I run this place on my own. Every now and then Rose fills in to give me a break. But she can only cover for me when the inn has no guests. Fortunately, she gets business regularly. Of course, if visitors want to stay overnight in Hutchins Creek, her inn is their only choice."

Both Jesse and Paige glanced toward the front window as Lulu started up and backfired.

"Henry uses quite a few southern expressions," Paige said. "Is he from around here originally?"

Jesse shook his head, not looking up. "No, but he's lived here a long time, since I was in my teens. That was more years ago than I want to think about."

"That explains the lack of southern accent," Paige said. "But was he originally from the South?"

"Not quite sure," Jesse said. "Seems he said something once about being from the Midwest, but I could be wrong. He's lived here so long he's a local as far as residents are concerned. He's just part of Hutchins Creek, always around and helping out. He's been especially helpful at the museum and to Rose, too. It's nice having someone who's willing to greet guests at the station and escort them to the inn."

"Yes, I certainly appreciated that when I arrived."

"Exactly," Jesse said. "Makes a visitor feel welcome."

"I'd say Sam makes a decent one-girl welcoming committee, too," Paige added. "She offers a friendly introduction to the back yard, cheerful and smiling all the time. Her behavior is contagious, makes visitors feel welcome to explore."

"She's a great kid," Jesse agreed. "Certainly fills my life with sunshine, gets my mind off these bills. She's always willing to help if I ask her to."

"Especially in that miniature train area," Paige said.

"Oh, yes. That's her area for sure. Sometimes I have to ask her to not be quite so territorial when guests come around. I've heard her ask people for a password to get into the yard. Most visitors think it's cute, but a few who take things too seriously get huffy."

Paige smiled. "She pulled that password stunt on me the first time I was here."

"And you managed to be admitted." Jesse smiled. "What password did you use?"

"I believe I used the word, 'railroad.'"

"That one will do it. So will 'train,' 'caboose,' 'museum,' and a basic 'please.'"

"I take it everyone gets in, then." Paige said.

"You bet."

"Stephen Porter has the best response," Jesse said. "He uses the password 'I'll give you a nickel to let me in.' Works like a charm every time."

"I'll bet it does." Paige laughed. "She's a clever girl, very sweet, too."

"Well, I'm biased, of course, but I agree with you. I sure wish her mom were still around to watch her grow up." Jesse sighed. "Cancer, when Samantha was just a year old."

"I'm so sorry," Paige replied. Until now, she hadn't known the specific reason Jesse's wife had passed away. She was glad he had both Rose and Lily to help out.

"We get by," Jesse said, looking up as the front door's whistle signaled another arrival.

Leaving Jesse to attend to the new visitors, Paige wished him a good day and returned to the inn.

CHAPTER TWENTY-FOUR

Paige set her coffee mug on a side table and looked across the inn's front parlor. Jake's book lay open on his chest as he inhaled and exhaled slowly, eyes closed. His late afternoon trip to Durango and back to inspect the horses had sapped his energy, so it was unsurprising that he'd dozed off while reading. He'd returned filled with enthusiasm, recounting the visit to the ranch, the excitement of working with and riding all three of the horses. The quarter horse and appaloosa had been gentle, with sweet dispositions, just as he'd expected. The Arabian also lived up to his initial suspicions, showing a feisty temperament, but not more than he could handle. Confident all three horses would be a good fit for his ranch, he'd arranged plans to purchase them and transfer them to Jackson Hole.

In turn, Paige had recounted her visit to the museum, her exploration of the caboose, the conversation with Jesse, and the accomplishment of finishing the railroad article and sending it off to Susan. She and Jake had both had long, productive days. Yet, while he was able to relax, she was energized, awake and restless.

She tiptoed back to the suite to grab a light jacket and jotted down a quick note to Jake to let him know she'd be back after a walk. Rose was setting up for the following morning's breakfast as Paige passed through the foyer, so she let her know, too, that she was going out for a bit. Sam followed Rose from one place setting to another, placing a napkin alongside each set of silverware.

"Take a flashlight," Rose said. "It's almost dark out there. You'll find one by the front door."

"Yes," Sam said, taking on Rose's adult tone. "Take a flashlight. It's smart to have a flashlight when it's dark."

"Thank you, Rose, and thank you, Sam. I won't be long." Paige picked up one of several flashlights propped up on a small table and headed out.

A nagging feeling that she'd missed something at the museum led her straight there. A glance at Jesse's house showed lights off, other than one bulb on the front porch. Apparently Jesse was out for the evening, which explained why Sam was at the inn helping Rose. The thought that Jesse might have plans pleased her. His wife had been gone for years already. Keeping the museum going in addition to raising a child alone wasn't easy. He deserved some personal time.

Reassured by the flashlight, she slipped through the back gate and made her way around the yard. Retracing her steps from that afternoon, Paige moved from one train car to another, directing the light at areas that someone could have tampered with in the past. One by one, she inspected each car's walls, floor and siding, moving on once satisfied there was nothing to discover.

Paige sat on the back steps of the museum and turned off the flashlight. It was no use continuing to search. If there had ever been coins stashed away at the museum, they'd surely have been discovered sometime over these ninety years.

The sound of a car drew Paige's attention out to the street. She knew no one could see her where she sat in the dark, but she could see the car that passed by under the dim street lights. She recognized it easily: Lulu. Assuming Henry was going to pull over, she stood and brushed dirt off her jeans, prepared to say hello. However, Lulu continued on. As the old car faded away, Paige sat back down and returned to her thoughts.

There wasn't even a guarantee that the coin Sam found was from the stolen batch. A visitor might have dropped it, or it may have been lost in one of the train cars long ago and fallen out after the car was moved to the museum. Sam, who was always exploring, might have found it somewhere else – at the inn, perhaps, or at the Rails Café – and brought it with her to the museum yard.

Again the sound of an engine interrupted her thoughts. Expecting it to be Henry again, Paige felt a shiver of fear run through her when she saw, instead, a tan car pulled up to the curb. Chancy! She had no desire to run into him alone, at night. Although in the first few moments she'd met him, he seemed like a fragile, old man, his robust reaction to the coin had scared her. She held her breath, hoping he would pull away from the curb and continue on, but, to her dismay, he turned off the ignition. When she heard a creaky car door opening, she quickly looked for a place to hide. The Morning Star was her closest option, so she made a beeline for it as she heard the car door swing shut.

Hovering behind a bench inside, she prayed she'd made it without Chancy seeing her. She remained motionless for several minutes, listening for footsteps, but heard nothing. Where would he have gone, if not inside the museum yard? To Jesse's house? No one was home. Besides, she had no reason to believe he knew Jesse personally. Inside the museum itself? Why would he have a key?

She inched up until she was able to peek out the train window and across to the Impala. It was still there. Wherever Chancy had gone, he'd be returning to the car at some point. As much as she wished she were back at the inn watching Jake's peaceful, sleeping expression, she couldn't risk moving.

Minutes passed without any sound, but then the soft scraping of footsteps on gravel strummed her nerves. She panicked when the sound of the footsteps grew closer instead of passing by or fading. She clutched the flashlight firmly, counting on the heavy, blunt object to deliver at least one good blow. Her grip tightened as she heard the person stop just outside the door. As a dark figured stepped aboard the train, she raised the flashlight over her head, prepared to strike.

"Paige?"

Motionless, she tried to release the terror she'd just been feeling. "Jake? Is that you?" she whispered.

"Yes, Paige, of course it's me." Jake boarded the train and walked down the aisle, finding Paige hovering behind a seat back. "What are you doing here?"

"Well, what are *you* doing here?" Paige lowered the flashlight. Her weak voice gained strength with each word.

"I saw your note. I knew you'd end up here."

Paige straightened up, but only long enough to grab Jake's hand and tug him behind the seat. She grasped his jacket and pulled him close.

"Cozy, but somewhat uncomfortable, Paige. If you're feeling affectionate, maybe we should go back to the inn."

Jake started to stand up, but Paige pulled him back down. "Chancy's here."

"What are you talking about?" Jake said. "No one is here."

"His car is parked on the street." Paige insisted.

"And that's why you're hiding in here?"

"Yes," Paige whispered.

"Paige, I think this whole coin thing has made you paranoid. So what if he's here. Maybe he drove down for a bite at the Rails Café or something. Maybe he has a friend in town and came to visit. I didn't see anyone in the yard. Let's go back to the inn. Maybe…a back massage might calm your nerves?"

Paige could hear the light teasing in Jake's voice. Admittedly, a massage sounded lovely. Being scrunched down and tense had strained every muscle in her body. Cautiously, she allowed Jake to stand and pull her to her feet. Almost convinced she had imagined being in danger, she followed Jake toward the door. But a burst of noise pierced the night air and a sharp jolt caused them to stumble and fall before they could leave The Morning Star.

"What was that?" Paige cried out over the noise.

"It sounded like an engine," Jake shouted. He attempted to stand up and help Paige to her feet, but a sudden movement threw them both off balance again.

"We're moving!" Paige said. "Someone must still be switching the cars around. I saw some had been shifted this morning."

"Is that normal?" Jake made another attempt to get them both to their feet, this time successful.

"I don't know!" Paige's panic grew stronger with every passing second. "Let's just get out of here." She edged forward, but Jake's strong grasp stopped her as she neared the door.

"We're moving too quickly!" he shouted. "It's not safe to jump." He pulled her away from the door and pushed her into a seat. "Stay there!" His command was firm – almost firm enough for Paige to listen. Instead, she followed him as he ran to the far end of the car, stepping out onto the back porch, where he attempted to turn a wheel for the emergency brake. A few choice words tumbled across his lips.

"What's wrong?" Paige shouted.

"I told you to stay put," Jake yelled back. Again he tried to turn the wheel. "It's stuck."

Paige could tell the car was gaining speed. She looked back to see the museum disappearing behind them, as well as the engine that had pushed the car forward. Worse yet, she could feel them moving ahead at a downhill angle.

"We're not attached to the engine anymore!" she screamed.

Jake braced his foot against a railing and leaned back, using all his body weight and strength to put pressure on the emergency brake. Paige was both terrified and hopeful. Still, the car continued to move forward, and the wheel refused to budge. Jake adjusted his grip and braced again, continuing to strain against the stubborn equipment.

"This is a long grade!" Paige shouted, her heart pounding inside her chest. With one hand grasping the back of the nearest seat, she cupped one hand in front of her mouth so that he could better hear her over the clattering of wheels over tracks. "We have to jump!"

"No!" Jake again changed angles, stabilizing his weight against a different railing in an attempt to put more leverage on the brake. This time the wheel gave way, sending Jake sprawling to the floor as he lost his balance. Paige screamed as he slipped toward the edge of the porch, just inches away from sliding off. He grabbed a railing and pulled himself back up, grasping the wheel again. Slowly the train began to slow down. Metal screeched against metal.

Although adrenalin continued to pump through her at a furious pace, Paige began to breathe more easily as the speed of the train diminished.

Jake continued to apply pressure to the brake, slowly bringing the train to a crawl. "Almost!" he shouted. "Another fifty yards or so and we'll be stopped."

Relieved the ordeal was almost over, Paige let go of the seat back and stepped forward toward Jake. But she staggered, then lost her balance altogether as a sudden jarring motion sent them both sideways. The car tilting steeply was the last movement Paige felt before everything went black.

CHAPTER TWENTY-FIVE

"Paige! Paige!" The words came to her as if through fog, almost indecipherable. They began as a distant murmur, like an echo against a mountain, and grew louder, like approaching thunder. Drawn out of a deep haze, Paige struggled to open her eyes, but couldn't muster the strength.

"Paige!"

Was that her name she was hearing? Paige wondered as the murky voice became clearer. *What was that striking her face?* She strained to open her eyes, succeeding this time, but saw only black. *Why can't I see?* Nothing made sense, not the voice, not the sharp sensation against her cheeks, not the darkness.

"Paige! Can you hear me?"

She turned her head slightly toward the voice, pain shooting across her left shoulder at the same time.

"Paige! It's Jake! Can you hear me?" the voice repeated. "Don't try to talk, just squeeze my hand if you can hear me."

Paige felt pressure on one hand and tried unsuccessfully to return it. Her fingers wouldn't move. *What was wrong? Something was terribly wrong.* The pressure moved to the other hand. This time she managed to wrap her fingers lightly around whatever pressed against her hand.

"Jake?" she whispered, suddenly frightened. "I can't see!"

"It's OK, Paige," Jake said. "It's dark; there's no light."

"No light?" Paige mumbled, confused. "Why is there no light?" She became aware that she was shivering. *It's so cold...*

"It's nighttime," Jake said. "We were in an accident. Here, this will help you stay warm."

Paige winced as something wrapped around her, some type of cloth, maybe? *Jake's jacket...* She tried to sit up, but pain stopped her. She gave up, her muscles melting into the hard ground.

"Don't try to move," Jake said. "We need to wait for help."

"Phone," Paige whispered. She fought to remember where she kept her phone, if she had it with her. As she searched her memory for the information, a rush of emotion overtook her as the events leading up to that moment filtered back into her mind. She felt herself begin to shake uncontrollably. She heard sobs coming from somewhere. Were they hers?

"In your left pocket? That's where you keep it."

Paige felt Jake reach into her pocket. Another sharp surge of pain swept through her as he slid the phone out. Her hip felt like it was on fire. Her left arm and shoulder felt like they were on fire. Yet she was shivering. The combination of everything seemed surreal.

"The phone is shattered," Jake said, "We can't use it."

"Yours?" Paige whispered.

"Gone. It was in my shirt pocket. It could have landed anywhere. It's OK, Paige; someone will find us."

Paige struggled to lift her right arm, succeeding in raising it halfway, her elbow lingering on the ground. It was enough to reach Jake's face. She touched his cheek with her fingers and gasped. "Is that...you're bleeding..."

"It's all right," Jake said. "It's just a cut, nothing serious."

"Help?" Paige mumbled. The words escaped her lips as half question and half confusion.

"Someone will find us. That crash had to have been loud, and we can't be more than a mile from Hutchins Creek, maybe not even that far." Jake's voice was reassuring, though Paige detected a hint of worry.

"Go...find..." Paige fought to focus.

"Absolutely not," Jake said. "I'm not leaving you alone out here to go get help, not in the dark and not after someone tried..." His voice faded away, unwilling to finish the sentence.

Again, Paige tried to sit up, but Jake stopped her. "You need to stay still until help arrives. You don't know what kind of injuries you have."

"You...?"

"Don't worry about me," Jake said. "We were both lucky. It could have been much worse. We landed clear of the train car."

"Clear of...how?"

"I...pushed you," Jake said.

Paige attempted to piece together this new information. Little by little, the episode was coming back to her. She lifted her head slightly off the ground, in spite of a shooting pain in her left shoulder. "You...pushed me?" Her voice became louder as the visual image formed. "You threw me off a train? A *moving* train? Seriously, Jake?"

"Stop trying to move!" Jake insisted. Placing his hands on each side of her face, he eased her head back down onto the ground. "Yes, of course I threw you off the train. It was heading for a cluster of trees and boulders. We could have ended up in the crash."

Attempting to take a deep breath, Paige felt a sharp pain in her ribcage and cried out. "It hurts when I breathe."

"Take shallow breaths," Jake advised. "You probably cracked a rib. Or two."

"Or three," Paige added, exhaling slowly.

"The flashlight," Jake said. "You had a flashlight with you. You were ready to knock me out cold with it. Maybe I can find it."

"Could have rolled anywhere."

"If I can find it, I might be able to locate my phone," Jake said. "There's a chance it could still work."

Paige heard a grunt from Jake as he stood, following by an expletive.

"What?"

"My ankle," Jake said. "I can't put all my weight on it. Must be sprained. I remember it twisting after I jumped, just before I landed on you."

"Not nearly as romantic as it sounds…"

"Tell me about it." Jake made another weak attempt to laugh, then grunted again. "I can still hop. I'm going to try to find the flashlight."

Sounds of crackling leaves and snapping twigs accompanied Jake's efforts to find the flashlight. A wave of fear hit Paige as she heard Jake moving farther away. When she tried to take deep, calming breaths, the sharp pain that radiated across her ribcage reminded her of the need to inhale lightly.

"Found it."

Jake's voice, though faint, sounded encouraging.

"Your phone?"

"No, the flashlight," Jake replied. "As good as, if not better than, finding the phone. Maybe we can figure out what happened even if the phone doesn't turn up." The crackling and snapping resumed as he made his way back to Paige. "Your right hand is fine, right? That's the one you moved before."

"Yes."

"Then can you hold the flashlight and aim it toward the train while I look?"

Jake helped Paige grasp the flashlight and balance it across her chest. She twisted her wrist from side to side, proving that she could direct the light so that Jake could search different sections of ground.

"Great," Jake said. "Now just hold onto it and only swing the light if I tell you to." He kissed Paige's forehead and hobbled off toward the train.

"How far away is the train?" Paige asked.

"About fifteen yards from here," Jake answered. "Far enough that we were thrown clear before it hit the side of the mountain." His voiced paused. "Twist the light a little more to the left."

Paige followed his directions, managing to twist her head enough to see Jake approaching the end of the train car.

"Here's the problem," Jake called back. "This metal device. It's a derailer."

"A derailer? What does that mean? We hit a section of track that branches off?"

"I'm afraid not, Paige," Jake said. "This was set on the tracks with the intention of derailing this train car."

"But trains come through here every day without problems. Which means…" She paused, putting the pieces together. "…That it was purposely put out here tonight, after the last train came through."

"That has to be right," Jake said. "Otherwise today's train would have had a problem."

Paige could hear the strain in Jake's voice, a sign his injured ankle was hurting him. She adjusted the light until she could see his stance. "You're putting more weight on that ankle than you should be," she warned. "Just come back and rest. Someone will find us."

"No," Jake said firmly. "I need to find the phone so we can call for help. This wasn't an accident."

"Not an accident," Paige repeated, absorbing the full meaning of the words. "So it was aimed at…?"

"The person most likely to be snooping around the train yard at night, Paige," Jake said. "Who do you think that might be?"

Even Paige couldn't deny Jake's reasoning. Clearly, she was the target.

"Shift the light to the right," Jake asked. "No, back a bit. I think I saw the cell phone under the car."

Paige heard Jake's words, but kept the stream of light focused where it had landed. She struggled to sit up, fighting against the searing pain in her shoulder, ribs and hip.

"Paige? The flashlight?"

"Jake," Paige said. "Forget the phone a minute. Look back where I'm pointing the flashlight."

"We need the phone, Paige, to call for help."

"Look behind you," Paige repeated, her voice forceful and pained at the same time. "Something's gleaming on the ground."

Jake moved toward the light and leaned forward to inspect the ground. "Well, I'll be..."

"Is it another coin?" Paige strained to move closer, but the pain was too severe.

"Yes, it is. But not just one, looks like there are three."

"Can you tell where they fell from? Better yet, can you help me move over to look?"

"No." Jake's voice was firm. "You're not moving. You're already injured. You'll just risk making it worse."

"Then tell me what you see!" Paige shifted the light, frustrated, hoping to see something from the distance.

"Move the light higher," Jake instructed.

"Is there a crack in the underside of the car?"

"It's hard to tell. But the car's leaning to the side, and the front is resting against a large boulder. Looks like it took a couple of trees out, too."

"Then they might have rolled out from inside." Paige grimaced, impatient that she couldn't search herself.

"Could be. I'm checking."

"Any floorboards cracked open?" Paige waited for an answer while Jake shuffled his weight around on his one good leg.

"Several, but nothing in them."

"That doesn't make sense," Paige said. "It can't be a coincidence that other coins are here. Sam wouldn't have been this far away from town when she found the other one."

"Wait, here's one more."

"Where?"

"Balanced inside the entryway."

"How far away from the ones on the ground?"

"Directly above them."

"Then look above there. Something must have cracked open when the car crashed."

"Shift the light higher," Jake said.

Paige refocused the light as Jake pulled himself up into the topsy-turvy car. A metallic creak rang out, startling her. She worried the car would fall, but the boulder held it up.

"Paige, I think I found it," Jake said. "There's a crack in the railing across one of the seats backs."

"The metal bar on the top?"

"Yep, exactly. And…I can feel more coins when I stick my fingers inside."

"So they were hidden in the train all along," Paige gasped. "But welded inside a seat back. No wonder no one found them after all these years. Except for Sam…how odd."

"Maybe not that odd," Jake said. "There's a tiny crack at the base of the seat back. One must have slipped out. Didn't you say she often played under the car?"

"Yes. I caught her crawling out of that spot a couple of days ago. I think she spends plenty of time there."

Jake slid out of the car. "Move the light back…no, more to the left…there, stop. I was right, that's my phone. And…it's working!"

"Great!" Paige breathed a painful sigh of relief. She closed her eyes, listening to a scuffling sound that she interpreted as Jake returning to her. "Call for help. Call…the inn. Yes, the inn. Rose will send someone out here."

"That won't be necessary," a familiar voice said.

CHAPTER TWENTY-SIX

Paige stared at the figure in front of her, stunned. Stephen Porter? Had he been after the coins all this time? All the years he'd been coming to stay at Rose Hutchins' inn? Was this his motive, not a fondness for Hutchins Creek or support for his son's interest in trains? What about Tommy? Why would he risk everything he had for this? The answer to these jumbled questions was simple: greed.

"Stephen?" Jake sounded as shocked as Paige. His voice grew stronger as he hobbled over to Paige's side. "What are you doing here?"

"It's obvious, don't you think?" Paige said. "He's after the coins. He has been all along."

"Is that true?" Jake asked.

Paige could hear how angry Jake was.

"Wait just a minute now. What are you talking about?" Stephen Porter stepped forward, and both Paige and Jake recoiled despite their injuries.

"You know exactly what we're talking about," Jake insisted. "You've been using your visits to Hutchins Creek as excuses to search for the cache of coins. You could have killed us with that runaway train car stunt." Jake grabbed the flashlight out of Paige's hand and wielded it like a club.

Stephen held up both hands and stepped back. "What stunt? I heard a crash and came down to see what happened. How badly are you injured?"

"Then why did you say it wouldn't be necessary to call for help?" Paige argued, ignoring the question. She winced as pain stung her ribcage.

"Because I already called 911 when I saw the crash from the road, before I even walked down here." The sound of approaching sirens backed him up. "Tell me what happened."

Paige glanced at Jake and then back to Stephen Porter. What was the point in not telling him? Either he already knew and was hiding it, or he really didn't have anything to do with the accident and was trying to help.

"Someone started up that switch engine and pushed The Morning Star forward." Paige waited for a response from Stephen.

"And?" Stephen stepped aside as two paramedics approached.

"Anyone else in the train car who might be injured?" The first paramedic asked, and then attended immediately to Paige while the other asked Jake if he was injured.

"I'm fine, just help her," Jake insisted. He turned back to Stephen. "Then the engine detached and backed off and left us in a free-fall." He tried to stand and move toward Paige, but winced as he attempted to put weight on the injured ankle. He sat back down at the request of the second paramedic, who handed him a bandage to hold against the cut on his forehead and cracked an ice pack and applied it to his ankle.

"Bad gash to the head and possible ankle fracture," the paramedic said to his partner.

"Multiple injuries here," the first paramedic replied. He'd taken Paige's vitals and checked her left shoulder, arm and hip. "We'll need the backboard to move her." He remained focused on Paige, but glanced quickly at Stephen. "You called this in?"

"Yes, I heard the crash from town. I'm staying at the inn and was out for a walk. I drove down and called as soon as I saw the train."

Paige listened to the activity around her, to the comments to and from Stephen, to the paramedic now telling her to relax, that she would be fine. Although she wanted to participate in the conversation, she followed directions, closed her eyes and relaxed. The initial panic and disorientation settled into an indescribable calm, a sense of release. She would get medical help, the pain would go away, and everything else could wait.

* * *

"Du...rangle? Drango?" Paige paused and tried again. "*Dur...ang...o?*"

"Yes, Paige. They brought you to Durango. Better medical facilities than in Hutchins Creek."

Jake's voice was soothing. He squeezed her right hand. When she looked at his face, she saw he was almost grinning.

"What?"

"You just sound cute," Jake said. "If you weren't in pain, it would be funny."

"Funny how?" *Wow, my voice sounds odd...*

"It's the pain meds, Paige," Jake explained. "They have you on a Dilaudid drip. You're a little out of it. OK, more than a little out of it." Now he truly grinned.

Paige nodded, still feeling a dull pain in her shoulder as she moved her head. "The IV, that feeling of fire in my neck."

"The nurse said that was common."

"...went away quickly," Paige said.

"Yes, she said it would."

"Your ankle?"

"Just a bad sprain, nothing to worry about."

"And...yur..." Paige paused and focused on her speech. "Your forehead?"

"A few stitches..."

"Two? Tree...I mean *three*? Sheesh." She had to fight to make the 'th' sound. Was her mouth filled with cotton?

"Fourteen," Jake admitted.

"The star..." Paige looked at Jake for information.

"The Morning Star isn't what you should be worried about, Paige. You need to focus on getting better," Jake said, his voice firm. "But amazingly, the damage was minimal. They'll fix the dents from the boulders and trees when they restore it."

Paige opened her eyes wider and tried to lift her head, but winced and gave up. "But the coins!"

Jake reached into his pocket and pulled out four, the three they'd found under the train, plus the one that teetered on the edge of the slanted floor inside. "I have these to send to the detectives at the Denver Mint."

"But..."

"They'll find the others when they inspect the car for repairs, Paige. This is enough to prove they were hidden in the car."

Jake stood up and stepped back, slipping the coins back into his pocket as a doctor entered the room.

"Hello Ms. MacKenzie, I'm Dr. Neal. I have your X-rays back from radiology."

"And?" Jake said.

Paige flopped a hand in Jake's direction, a sign to relax and listen.

"You dislocated your elbow and also have an acromioclavicular joint separation."

"'Glish...," Paige muttered. "*English*..."

"You separated your collar bone from your scapula, most likely from landing on your shoulder when you fell. You tore ligaments, but fortunately it's only a Grade 2 injury. You won't need surgery, but you'll need to wear a sling for a few weeks and then go through physical therapy to work on range of motion and strength."

"What about the elbow?" Jake ignored Paige when she tried again to get him to quiet down.

The doctor replied to Jake's question with a kind, yet professional smile. "Nothing that we can't fix. We're waiting for a room in order to reduce it."

"Re...duce?" Paige murmured.

"To put it back in place," Dr. Neal explained. "You also cracked a rib, but that will heal itself. I'll give you some anti-inflammatory medication and a soft ice pack that you can keep in your freezer and use for relief. And we'll put a couple of stitches in that cut on your hip."

"Then we can leave?" Paige asked. "I have suff...*stuff* I need to do. Fine out...I mean, *find* out."

Dr. Neal looked at Jake and smiled. "She's a tough one, hmm?"

Jake laughed and winked at Paige. "You have no idea."

CHAPTER TWENTY-SEVEN

Paige and Jake eased themselves into Lulu, grateful to Henry for being Hutchins Creek's unofficial town driver. Paige settled in the front seat, left arm and sling resting lightly on her stomach.

"Well, you two are a mighty fine sight," Henry said, "if I do say so myself. And I do. You with your sling, Ms. MacKenzie, and you back there with your crutches." He glanced over his shoulder at Jake. "That forehead of yours looks like it'll be a mite sore for a while, too." As he fired Lulu up and pulled away from the curb, he apologized to Paige when she winced at the movement.

"Thanks for picking us up, Henry," Paige said. "I'm sorry you had to go to through all this trouble."

"The way I see it, you two are the ones who've been through trouble. All I did was drive here to Durango. You're both lucky you weren't hurt worse. How'd you end up in the middle of this mess, anyway?"

"I was just looking for more of...Sam's 'birds,' honestly," Paige said. "Coins like the one she found before. I felt sure there were more, somewhere in the museum yard, at least." Paige remained silent for a few minutes, still exhausted from the ordeal. Conversation was more physically taxing than she expected.

"I still can't believe The Morning Star got loose like that," Henry said. "It's always secured properly."

"Well, it wasn't last night," Jake said.

"Did they get it back up the track?" Paige asked.

"Sure did," Henry said. "Jesse pulled it back up the grade this morning, nice and early. Had to. It would have blocked the Durango-Silverton morning run."

"How much damage?" Paige slowly turned her head toward Henry despite the pain.

"A couple of big dents and some scratches along the sides and top. It can be repaired. We'll just have to keep building that restoration fund. Might take longer to raise enough."

Paige felt herself growing impatient for details. "Henry, what did they find out about the derailer?"

Henry turned toward Paige, his expression puzzled. "The derailer?"

"The one that had been placed on the track," Jake said. "Any way they can identify where it came from?"

"Jesse didn't say anything about a derailer," Henry said, shaking his head. "And I was there when he brought The Morning Star back into the yard. I'm sure he would have mentioned it. Maybe you folks mistook some other mechanical part for one of those."

Paige watched Jake's face in the rear view mirror. He was clearly as confused as Paige was now. Yet Henry had to be the one who was mixed up. *No derailer?*

"No, Henry." Jake leaned forward in the back seat. "I've been around railroad yards before. There was definitely a derailer. That's what caused The Morning Star to leave the track and hit those boulders."

"Kind of odd Jesse wouldn't mention that," Henry said.

"Yes, odd indeed," Paige agreed. She turned her head slowly toward the passenger window and remained quiet, watching the pine trees as the car continued north toward Hutchins Creek, until the next obvious question hit her.

"What about the coins?"

Henry threw Paige another confused look. "What coins?"

"The coins…" Paige suddenly stopped herself. Something didn't feel right. She changed tactics. "Oh, just the coins I was hoping to find. It's not important."

To her relief, silence fell in the car, Jake remaining quiet, Henry focused on driving. She had enough to process without any more information – or *misinformation*, as it seemed.

* * *

"Someone's lying."

Jake took a drink of Iced Trestle Tea as he contemplated Paige's statement. She could see it in his eyes: he agreed. She could also see he was more worried about her than about unraveling town secrets or finding missing coins. As soon as Henry had dropped them off at the inn, he'd stated that it was time to leave Hutchins Creek. The six-hour nap he took after his restless night at the hospital didn't change his mind. Not even his comfortable spot at the Rails Café had affected his decision.

"You know it's not in my nature to leave something like this alone," Paige continued. "Aren't you curious? Who's hiding something here? Jesse? Stephen? Henry? Even Rose? And what about Chancy? I *did* see his car drive by the museum last night."

"Sure, I'm curious. But there are too many suspects, too much danger," Jake said. "Don't you have a plane flight booked tomorrow, anyway? Your Old West railroad article is done. And we've enjoyed being together all week, though I'd say last night was questionable."

"I agree," Paige said. It was ridiculous not to admit he was right. About everything, especially the fact that the previous night was far from ideal. "Still, humor me for a minute. Which of those five would be capable of starting up a switch engine?"

"You're not talking about motives?"

"No," Paige said. "I'm just talking capabilities and knowledge." She glanced around to make sure nearby tables were empty, and then lowered her voice. "Obviously Jesse. He grew up in a railroad family. He's been moving train cars around the yard for all those years since his father died. And you know he was out last night. Rose was watching Sam."

"Yes, Paige, I'm sure he knows how to move the exhibits around, including the engines and cars," Jake said. "But that doesn't mean…"

"I know," Paige interrupted. "It doesn't necessarily make him guilty of anything. But is it reasonable those coins could have been there for decades, and he didn't know? Didn't even look for them?"

"Maybe he didn't even know they existed. He didn't seem overly interested in the coin Sam found."

"True," Paige admitted. "Certainly he wasn't aware of the value. Not as hard as he's been trying to raise money to restore The Morning Star."

"Stephen, on the other hand, showed up almost immediately after the crash." Jake flagged the server down for an iced tea refill.

"Yes," Paige said. "At the very least, that seemed like remarkable timing."

"But you're getting off track here – ohh, sorry about the pun, that was bad," Jake said. "Why would Stephen know how to start up an engine?"

"He probably wouldn't, but we can't be sure of that. He's been coming to Hutchins Creek for years, and he hangs out around the museum. Maybe he's using Tommy's interest in trains as an excuse. Though I hate to think that." Paige sat back and thought about this. "Still, he probably had plenty of opportunities to watch Jesse."

"We have no way to know that," Jake pointed out. "And he seemed genuinely concerned last night when he found us after the accident."

"True," Paige whispered. "Still, it seemed odd that he was right there, just after it happened."

"Yes, but his explanation made sense, and the paramedics were right behind him."

"OK, OK," Paige said. "What about Henry?"

"Just a friendly and harmless town fixture, from what I can tell. A little eccentric, sure seems willing to help people out."

"I agree," Paige said. "I can't see Henry causing any trouble."

"And he didn't seem to know anything about the derailer or the coins aside from what he might have learned from us," Jake added.

"Maybe the coins were gone by the time they brought The Morning Star back up to the yard," Paige said. "Someone else could have removed them after we left with the paramedics."

"Or he could be lying when he says he didn't see them," Jake said. "And he's always been a part of Hutchins Creek, right? He's got that reputation for being helpful; maybe he's helped Jesse move those train cars around."

"Actually, he hasn't always lived here," Paige pointed out. "He came here about forty years ago."

"Really? I just assumed he was a local."

Paige shook her head. "No, Jesse said something about him coming in from the Midwest. He's not exactly sure where Henry came from originally. In fact, that seems sort of odd, now that I think about it. How do you not find out where someone is from, over that long a period of time? And he sure seems to know the train cars well."

"Like I said before: too many suspects and too much danger. Paige, please let this go. Tonight let's just enjoy a nice, relaxed evening together." Jake finished his iced tea and waited for her to respond.

"Fine."

"We'll send the other coins we collected to the detectives at the Denver Mint and let them take things from there."

"Fine."

"If you're hungry later, we can go down to The Iron Horse and have a quiet meal."

"Rose is making dinner."

"Good, even better," Jake said. "You see how easy this is? We don't need to go anywhere or worry about anything. We'll just relax at the inn."

Paige thought a moment and then smiled. "That sounds perfect."

"Great, we agree." Clearly pleased, Jake stood and retrieved his crutches from beside the booth, positioning his weight over his good ankle. He pulled his wallet out, tossed money on the table to cover both their check and a tip for the server, and put his wallet away.

Paige stood and accepted Jake's extended arm carefully with her one free hand. She walked toward the café exit, Jake hobbling right behind her. If he'd been able to see her face, he would have noticed that her smile lingered. Their last night in Hutchins Creek promised to be intriguing, especially since Jesse, Stephen and Henry, three of their "suspects," would all be there to share the meal Rose would fix.

CHAPTER TWENTY-EIGHT

"More cornbread?"

Paige smiled at Rose, tempted, but shook her head. "I won't be able to eat anything else if I fill up on bread. I've already had two pieces, complete with honey butter."

"No one can resist that honey butter," Jesse said. "Rose is famous around these parts for that particular concoction."

"It's the only reason I come around for meals," Henry quipped.

"Why, Henry Sanders!" Rose placed a square of cornbread on his plate. "I thought you were partial to my apple pie."

"Of course I am, Rose," Henry said. "It's hard to not be partial to anything you make."

"And here I thought it was just my charming personality."

"That, too, of course." Henry thanked Rose and reached straight for the butter crock.

Sam and Tommy skipped into the room and slid into seats. After they both held up their hands to prove they'd washed them, Jesse and Rose nodded their approval.

"Dad said he'd be here in a minute," Tommy said. "He's on the phone."

"OK, dear." Rose said.

"How're you two feeling?" Jesse asked Paige and Jake.

"Sore," Jake answered. The others around the table smiled sympathetically. "Paige got the worst of it, I'm afraid."

"I'm so glad your injuries weren't even worse," Jesse said. "I don't understand how the whole accident could have happened. I keep those cars secured. And the engine…"

"Jesse," Rose interrupted. "I don't think Paige and Jake want to relive those moments. They were terrifying enough to go through once, I'm sure."

"No, it's fine," Paige said.

"Are you sure?"

"Yes," Paige said. "I'm curious how it might have happened, too."

"All right, then," Rose said before she left to collect more of the meal.

"Could anyone start up that engine, Jesse?"

"Not just anyone, but it's not that hard. It only takes someone who's been around train yards enough to learn how."

"What about the coins?" Paige addressed the question to Jesse, but quickly had the attention of the whole table.

"What coins?" Jesse said.

"That's what I said on the way back from Durango," Henry piped up, looking at Jesse. "They asked me the same thing."

"You must have been mistaken," Jesse said. "I inspected the car when we dragged it back up to the yard. There was nothing there."

Paige and Jake exchanged glances.

"Jesse, I know what I saw," Jake said, his tone even.

"Saw what?" Rose asked, returning from the kitchen with a platter of fried chicken. Without waiting for an answer, she made a second trip and added serving bowls of mashed potatoes and sweet corn. She looked around the room, immediately picking up on the tension. "Wait just a minute. I'll have no serious discussions around my dinner table, especially with guests here. Now you all just decide if you want to go hungry or enjoy a nice meal."

"I choose a nice meal," Henry said as he rubbed his hands together.

"That's what I thought," Rose said.

"And the derailer?" Paige asked Jesse. "Maybe you didn't see the coins, but what about the derailer on the track?"

"We didn't find a derailer when we went down to the scene to drag the car back up to the yard," Jesse said.

"Yeah, I told 'em that, too," Henry said. "You sure you two weren't just imagining things in the dark?"

Paige placed her good hand on Jake's wrist. She was impressed that he stayed so calm when he answered.

"Jesse, I saw it, I know I did," Jake said, his tone even. "I inspected the tracks after we were thrown off."

"Sorry to be late. What did I miss?" Stephen slid into his chair and unfolded his napkin, placing it in his lap. He looked around the table and frowned.

"Nothing," Jesse said, passing him the basket of cornbread.

The platters of chicken and accompanying dishes circled the table, each guest filling a plate.

"We were asking about the coins inside The Morning Star," Paige said.

"There were coins inside The Morning Star?" Stephen asked. He took a square of cornbread from the basket.

Jesse set his fork down and looked at Stephen. "There weren't when I inspected it." He paused. "But you were the first on the scene. You didn't see any?"

Stephen shook his head. "I just called the paramedics. Once they arrived, I came back up to tell you about the crash. I never looked inside the car." He reached for a pat of butter with his knife. His voice struck Paige as oddly controlled considering Jesse's question had vaguely resembled an accusation.

"But you know about the coins," Paige said. "You knew about the stolen batch, even before we came back from the Denver Mint."

"That's true," Stephen said. "Jerome told us about them."

"Us?" Jesse asked.

"Isn't that right, Henry?" Stephen said.

All eyes turned to Henry.

"Well, yes. I guess there's no harm in saying so now," Henry said. "Seems just about everyone knows. Funny how Jerome sounded so 'hush hush' about the whole thing, considering how many people knew about it."

"You're talking about the theft itself?" Paige said. "Who else knew about that?" She waited as eyes flitted around the room, each person searching the others' faces.

"I knew," Jesse said. "Jerome took me out fishing one afternoon and told me. Said Jasper had hidden the coins somewhere."

"Jerome didn't say where?" Jake asked. "Did he know?"

Jesse shrugged. "Jasper never told him where they were hidden."

"He didn't want them to be found, I take it," Paige said.

"True, but not for the obvious reason, which would be to hang onto them."

"Why then?" Paige was growing more curious by the moment. Each added bit of information just brought new questions.

"The way I understood it from Jerome, Jasper was involved in the theft, but immediately regretted it," Jesse said. "He wanted to turn the coins back in, but his partner threatened to blame the entire caper on him. He would have gone down for the crime while the co-conspirator walked away free."

"So he hid them until he felt it was safe to turn them in," Stephen said.

Jesse nodded. "Right. That was his intention. But years passed by and it never seemed like the right time."

"And when Roosevelt recalled the gold, he felt he couldn't turn in stolen coins without repercussions." Jake said.

"That would make sense to me," Paige pointed out. She got a few confused looks. "In 1933 he was newly married with a baby on the way. Who would've taken care of Pearl and the baby if he went away? He must have told her he turned them in. That's why Pearl thinks Roosevelt has the coins. That's what she told us, anyway."

"I think eventually he would have turned them in if he hadn't passed away first. Or at least told Dad they were hidden in The Morning Star," Jesse said.

"He always guarded that car carefully," Henry said quietly.

Jesse turned to Henry, confused. "What did you say?"

"Your father, he guarded that car with his life."

"How do you know that? He never mentioned anything about guarding it to me."

Henry paused, aware he had the attention of the entire room now. "Because I used to ride the rails. Did it for many years. Learned from my old man. He was a hobo way back, was even crazy enough to 'ride the rods' underneath the cars. Died that way, too. I played it safe, sticking to boxcars and sliding into a passenger car now and then, when I could get away with it. I'd always try to sneak my way into The Morning Star if I was riding the Antonito-Durango line, way back when it still ran."

Paige gasped. "You're the one who marked the car, aren't you? With the hobo code?"

"The what?" Steven said, leaning forward.

"I can explain," Henry said. "Like I said, I'd try to sneak onto The Morning Star when I could. Usually I got away with it. But Jerome caught me once and threw me off. Threatened to come after me with a gun if I ever set foot on that car again. I put that mark on the train so others would know to stay away. I never saw him shoot at anyone, but that didn't mean he wouldn't."

"Jerome never recognized you later when you came to Hutchins Creek?" Jake asked.

Henry shook his head. "He'd only seen me that one time, and I was just a youngin' back then. Anyway, over the years I heard about the missing coins – you know how those hoard stories get around – and came here to see if there was anything to it. I got thinking about how Jerome would throw people off that train car. Then, once I was here, I found out how adamant he was about not having the train restored. I figured he was guarding something and maybe that something could be the coins."

"Henry," Jesse said. "You've been here for years. Have you been looking for those coins all this time?"

"At first I did, looked all around The Morning Star. Never found them. But then I realized I'd found something more valuable."

"Pirate treasure!" Tommy's shout caused everyone to jump since they'd been so caught up in Henry's story that they'd forgotten about the children, who had been oddly quiet until this point.

"No," Henry said, a smile creeping across his face. "Something even better than pirate treasure, Tommy."

"Wow, must be pretty special." Tommy and Sam looked at each other.

"It is," Henry said. "You see, when you live a hobo's life, you don't really have a place to call home. You don't have a regular joint for your morning coffee like the Rails Café. And you meet people, but they're always moving on. Here in Hutchins Creek I found a home, and a community. You can't put a price tag on that."

A commotion at the front door interrupted the discussion. The door opened and closed; heavy footsteps sounded. To the surprise of all but one person, Detectives Ferguson and Simons entered the room. Everyone was unnerved when they saw Chancy Conroy with them, Detective Simon's hand fastened on his upper arm.

"Found Mr. Conroy here lurking outside the museum," Detective Ferguson said.

"Chancy?" Jesse frowned. "I thought I told you a long time ago to stay away. The last time you pried a panel off the side of a train car, I had to pay Henry a Boxcar Burger to get him to fix it."

"Hey, if that lady can snoop around my shop, I can snoop around this here museum and inn." Chancy pointed at Paige.

"I knew I saw someone look out of that window," Paige whispered to Jake.

"Chancy worked here, way back, helped with chores in the yard," Jesse said. "There were quite a few episodes of vandalism back then – boards dislodged, the ground dug up. I suppose you were looking for the coins?"

"Never found anything," Chancy said. "I'd given up on them even being in this area until these people showed up with the Double Eagle they found." He nodded toward Paige and Jake.

"Was this back when you carried green and brown sweatshirts, Jesse?" Paige asked.

"Maybe," Jesse said. "Why do you...oh, wait." He turned to face Chancy, fuming. "You've been down in Durango bothering Pearl?

"Says who?" Chancy struggled to pull out of Simons' beefy grip.

"You left an old museum sweatshirt there," Paige explained. "The nursing home called here, thinking we'd left it when we went to visit her. But it was brown. The museum doesn't carry that color anymore."

"So what if I went to see her?" Chancy snarled. "Never did get any information out of that crazy old bag, anyway. And it's not like I was trespassing. Visitors are welcome there, you know."

"However, it *is* trespassing to enter the museum yard at night without permission," Detective Ferguson said.

"You aren't keeping those coins, Jesse," Chancy continued, ignoring the detective. "Those belong to me. If your grandfather hadn't hidden them from my father, this would have been settled long ago. They were supposed to be in on that together. Jasper back-stabbed my father when he hid them."

Paige noticed the puzzled faces around the room and explained. "Frank Conroy was a guard at the Denver Mint at the time the coins went missing."

"They cleared him." Chancy stomped a foot.

"For lack of evidence," Detective Ferguson pointed out.

"Jasper only hid the coins in order to give them back to the Denver Mint, where they should have stayed all along," Jesse added. "In any case, it doesn't matter. There aren't any coins."

"There *are* coins," Paige insisted. "Someone is just hiding them." She paused and looked around the room. "Again."

"Paige is right. The coins are here," Stephen said. "Or Detectives Ferguson and Simons wouldn't have made the trip out from Denver."

"*You!*" Chancy barked at Stephen. "You were supposed to be helping me."

"Actually, it was the other way around," Stephen said. "You were helping me, you just didn't know it."

"I was going to cut you in."

"Which would have been very generous of you," Stephen added. "Except for two small details: One, the coins don't belong to you. And, two, I've been working with the Denver Mint to help recover them. You weren't the only one who thought it was convenient that I often stay in Hutchins Creek."

"Cool! My dad's a spy!" Tommy jumped out of his seat. Stephen prompted him to sit back down.

"Is this true?" Jesse asked.

"No. I'm not a spy," Stephen said, turning to Jesse apologetically. "Please don't think I was taking advantage of your family's hospitality. I'd been coming here long before the Mint Police asked me to keep them informed."

"So where are the coins?" Detective Ferguson directed the question to the room in general. "Seems everyone here knows about them, yet no one knows where they are now."

"I have them."

CHAPTER TWENTY-NINE

Rose stood in the doorway, a small bag in her hand.

"It's time for this almost century-old situation to be laid to rest," Rose said. "The coins are going back to the Denver Mint, where they belong."

"But how did you even know the coins were there?" Jesse asked.

"I always suspected they were hidden in The Morning Star, but had no idea exactly where. I removed them when the car was first pulled back up behind the museum," Rose added. "While you were still inspecting the tracks."

"What exactly was Jasper's job when he left Denver to work on the railroad?" Paige asked.

"He was a welder," Rose said. "Worked in the railroad yard out of Antonito."

"A welder?" Paige looked at Jake, who nodded. "That explains why they were hidden in the metal backing of the seat."

Rose stepped forward and handed the bag of coins to the detectives. "I believe it's time for you to have these."

"And I have these to add," Jake said. He pulled four coins from his pocket and turned them over to the detectives. "These fell from The Morning Star when it crashed. I planned to notify you, but it looks like Stephen beat me to a phone call."

Detective Ferguson took the bag from Rose, poured the contents on the table, and counted the coins, adding in the ones that Jake had handed him. He then took a notebook from his pocket, flipped it open and checked his notes. "Looks like you have 32 coins altogether."

"That's right," Rose said. "That's everything."

"You're not suggesting we're keeping some, are you?" Jesse asked.

Detective Ferguson smiled, glanced at his partner, who also smiled. "No, nothing like that." He checked the coins again, as well as his notebook.

Paige leaned forward, curious. "What do you mean?"

"Our notes regarding the 1926 theft show that twenty-six coins went missing."

"So...these aren't the stolen coins?" Jesse asked, confused. "Is that what you're saying?"

"Not exactly," Detective Ferguson said. "I'm certain these are the stolen coins, at least twenty-six of them are. But the other six may well have been a legitimate purchase by your grandfather."

"Meaning..." Jesse stood up and walked over to the coins, taking a closer look.

"Meaning that six of these belong to your family," Detective Simons explained. "We came out here to collect twenty-six coins. That's the number we'll be taking back."

"Confound it," Chancy shouted, stomping his foot again. "Those are in top condition! They're worth a good fifteen grand each!"

"Yet you tried to buy one from us for five hundred dollars?" Jake said.

Chancy shrugged. "A guy's got to make a living, you know."

"I don't think you'll need to worry about that now," Detective Ferguson said, pulling out handcuffs and securing Chancy's wrists. "I think your living expenses will be covered for some time."

"What are you talking about?" Chancy sputtered. He struggled against the metal cuffs unsuccessfully.

"It seems there was a little accident here last night." Detective Ferguson glanced at the sling on Paige's arm and then back at Chancy. "Do you happen to know anything about that?"

"Of course not!" Chancy twisted against the detective's firm grasp. "All right, all right, I was in the museum yard last night. But I wasn't trying to hurt anyone. I just meant to scare that nosy reporter away before she found the coins."

"Are you an idiot?" Jake suddenly shouted, jumping to his feet. "Do you realize you could have taken away the woman I love? Her future? My future? Our future life? Our future children? Everything that matters to me. To us?"

Paige felt a slow warmth spread through her as Jake's words landed in her heart. For a moment the entire room disappeared. All she saw was a man who was everything she'd ever hoped for.

"So you removed the blocks that secure the car? And then put the derailer on the track so the train couldn't pick up speed when you bumped it into motion?" Henry's question to Chancy brought Paige's attention back to the scene unfolding around her.

"Well, it didn't get very far, did it? Besides, I never did start the engine up. When I got back to the museum, I heard it start up from outside the gate. I went back to get the derailer, but the train had already run off the track. I picked it up after the ambulance left."

"Before I got there," Jesse said. "That's why I didn't see it."

"Right," Chancy said. "So, you see, I'm not guilty. You can let me go now, detectives."

"No so fast," Ferguson said. "You were still guilty of planning it. We'll be discussing this at the local station."

"Then who *did* start the engine up?" Paige looked around the room. Jake, Jesse, Rose, Henry and Stephen all looked around, as well. Only two heads remained still, both staring silently into laps.

"Sam? Tommy?" Jesse asked. "Do you know something you're not telling us?"

The children glanced at each other, but kept their heads down. Tommy elbowed Sam, who returned the gesture.

"Tommy," Stephen said firmly. "Speak up. What do you kids know? Did you see something? You need to tell us."

Tommy looked up, his voice barely a whisper. "We were just playing…"

"What do you mean, just playing?" Jesse asked. He leaned forward.

"Like *we* do sometimes, Dad," Sam said, finally looking up, too. "When you move the cars around and let me sit by you."

"Yeah, we were playing train," Tommy said. "Sam was showing me how."

"But then it made that rumbling noise, and there was a bump," Sam explained. "We got scared and ran back here."

"Well, I'll be," Henry said, shaking his head. "The kids bumped that train into motion."

"Only because the accident was already set up," Jesse added. "But that's not the point."

"No," Stephen agreed. "They shouldn't have been playing in the train without supervision."

"We didn't know the engine rolled forward, Dad! We didn't mean to bump anything! We ran and ran because we were scared!"

"I think you two will skip dessert," Rose said quickly. "You may be excused. We don't need to waste the detectives' time on this. You'll discuss it later with your fathers."

Sam and Tommy stood up, faces tear streaked, and dashed out of the room. Paige could hear Sam sobbing.

"I think our job here is done," Detective Simons said, steering Chancy toward the front door. "You're going with us, for more questioning."

Detective Ferguson spread the coins out, asked Jesse and Rose to pick out six to keep. They chose six, all in mint condition. The detective bagged the rest, said goodbye and left.

"This should go a long ways toward restoring The Morning Star," Rose said, looking around the room.

"It'll just about do it," Jesse said. "According to the estimates I have."

A small voice chimed into the conversation.

"Miss Paige? Mr. Jake? We didn't know we got you hurt. We're really sorry."

Sam stood in the doorway and held out her hand, which clutched a stack of bills. "Will this make it better? Will this help with The Morning Star?"

Jesse walked over to her, taking the money from her outstretched arms. "Where did you get this?"

"I saved it," Sam said. She sniffled. "You always say to set a little bit aside from everything you make."

"Yes," Jesse said. "Saving is a good idea. But you don't work, Sam. Where did you get the money to save?"

"I do, too, work," Sam insisted. "We work together when people come to visit the museum."

"That's right," Rose jumped in. "I've seen you and Sam behind the counter together, Jesse. She 'helps you' sometimes, remember? Like when you have to go into the back room to help a conference group? Or step out on the back porch to answer a visitor's question?"

"Ah, yes," Jesse said as the situation began to make sense. "And you've helped me give change to customers before, haven't you, Sam?

"Yep, I'm a good helper."

"Yes, you are," Rose sighed. "So The Morning Star can look pretty like the little one inside."

"Well, thank you, Sam," Jesse said, taking the money. "I think we'll need to talk about doing this saving bit together from now on, as well as a few other things, like playing inside the trains."

"OK," Sam said. She turned to leave, but stopped and looked back at the adults in the room. "Was Great-Grandpa Jasper a bad guy? Because he took the coins?

"No, I don't think your great-grandpa was a bad guy." Rose stepped forward and took Sam's hands. "Sometimes people do something foolish and regret it later. We all make mistakes. Don't you think so, Sam? Do you understand what I'm saying?"

"Yes, Auntie Rose," Sam said quietly. "I understand."

CHAPTER THIRTY

Moonlight drifted through the gazebo's lattice roof as Paige and Jake set two steaming mugs of coffee on the table and sat down.

"I'm going to miss this gazebo," Paige sighed. "It's a perfect place to relax in the evening."

"Is that all you'll miss?" Jake wrapped one arm around Paige and kissed the top of her head as she settled against him.

"Could be," Paige teased. She winced as she searched for a position that wouldn't interfere with her sling.

"Does your arm feel any better today?"

"Not much," Paige admitted. "But I talked to my doctor this morning, in New York. After I keep it immobile for a couple weeks, she'll check it and give me some exercises to get it back in shape. The hospital in Durango sent the X-rays to her."

Jake nodded, but remained quiet.

"What?" Paige looked at Jake's face, his expression unreadable.

"Nothing," Jake said. "I just forget sometimes that you have a life back East. I only see the work side of your life out here – the articles, your conversations with your editor, all that. But you have more than a career there. You have a history, a place you live, familiar people, doctors you trust, a favorite coffee shop…"

"Deli," Paige clarified.

"OK, deli." Jake paused. "They don't serve a good rack of BBQ ribs, do they?"

"Unlikely."

"Or have a pig roast on Monday nights?"

"A *what?*"

"Anyway," Jake continued. "I need to stop overlooking all that."

"You've only seen me outside that everyday life," Paige said. "But…"

Jake sat up, reached for his coffee. "It's fine, Paige, really. I understand." His tone was soft and accepting.

"I don't think you do…" Paige shifted to face Jake.

"All I want, above everything, is for you to be happy."

"Well, I…"

"And if that means you stay in New York, and I only get to see you some of the time, I can deal with that. I'm just glad you're in my life. You make the world…"

"A little crazier?" Paige grinned. She knew exactly what she planned to say, but if Jake wasn't going to slow down long enough to let her speak, she might as well stretch it out and torment him.

Jake smiled. "No doubt a little crazier. Life is never boring around you. Just trying to keep you out of trouble is a challenge."

"Yes, I imagine so." Paige took a sip of her coffee, contemplating her next words. "I've been thinking, seeing as your life is so boring and all that…"

"Oh, it's fine," Jake said quickly, his tone resigned. "I have the ranch to work on. There's so much to do to get it ready for guests. Not to mention setting down firm business goals in writing, and getting a marketing plan together."

"It sounds like you'll need some help," Paige ventured. She watched casually as he paced back and forth. *I'm having way too much fun seeing this play out*, she thought.

"Sure, but there are great resources in Jackson. I can hire a contractor to plan out the cabin remodels, and a company for marketing."

"You'll also need to put together a media kit," Paige added. "You know, for announcements about the ranch, an article for the local paper, that kind of thing…"

Jake nodded, still pacing as he thought through the plans. "Yes, I'm sure the *Jackson Hole News & Guide* will want information."

"I imagine so." Paige relaxed against the loveseat's cushion and took a sip of coffee.

"And I'll have to set up a website."

"Absolutely."

"And have professional photography done."

"No question."

"There's a lot to do." Jake took a deep breath.

"It certainly sounds like it," Paige said. "It would be much easier with help, wouldn't it?"

"I'll be able to pull a good team together."

"I'm sure you will," Paige said. "But I was thinking it might help to have someone right by your side. Or at least in close proximity."

"Like an assistant? To handle daily activity, phone calls, that sort of thing?"

"I was thinking more along the lines of someone who knows how to make excellent coffee, *and* write press releases for the daily paper."

Jake sat back down beside Paige and looked into her eyes, all business talk forgotten.

"What are you saying, Paige?"

"I think you know what I'm saying," Paige laughed. "Now that I finally have your attention. It's a little hard to get a word in edgewise, between your business plans and your insistence that you'll be fine if I stay in New York."

"I would find a way to be fine, if that's what you needed to be happy."

Paige reached forward with her good arm and ran her fingers through Jake's hair. "You're a wonderful man, you know? I don't know how I was lucky enough to meet you."

"I think you mean clumsy enough," Jake whispered, leaning forward to give Paige a kiss.

"You bumped into me," Paige whispered back, recalling their first meeting in the Jackson library.

Jake shook his head. "I think it was the other way around."

Paige smiled, knowing this was a routine they would continue to toss around in the future whenever their initial meeting came up in conversation.

"But you still haven't told me where I can find this perfect assistant," Jake said. "The one who can make great coffee *and* write a press release. I want to hear it. You're just torturing me now. Where do I find this amazing person?"

Paige looked around the gazebo, nonchalant. "I think you'll need someone from outside of Jackson, outside of Wyoming, even."

"I don't know, Paige. Why would someone want to move to Jackson Hole? Aside from the spectacular scenery, clean air and rich history, that is?"

"Maybe because this person is in love with a handsome cowboy and wants to be closer to him, because he makes her life feel complete."

"I like the sound of that," Jake said. "Do I know who this person is?"

"You might," Paige teased, then became serious. "I've thought about it for some time, since you first asked me to think about moving to Jackson Hole, maybe even since I first met you."

"You don't say," Jake said, grinning.

"I *do* say, but I still have to arrange a lot of details, and talk to Susan to see if I might still be able to do some long-distance articles for *The Manhattan Post*. At least I could continue the series on the Old West, if she's open to that."

"I don't see why she wouldn't be. You need to travel out West for each article, anyway."

"I agree," Paige said. "But that's up to her."

"You could just make coffee and ride horses every day."

"I could, but…"

"But I would never ask you to give up your work," Jake said. "Or anything else that makes you who you are."

"Like my crazy adventures?"

"I don't think that would be possible, anyway," Jake laughed. "They seem to find you, wherever you go."

"True," Paige admitted. She turned sideways, curling up in Jake's arms. She felt safe, secure, and hopeful. No decision she'd ever made felt as right as this one.

Jake pulled Paige close, rested his head against the top of hers. A few moments of silence passed as each thought over the move that would bring them closer together. Jake was the first to speak. "I have just one question, then."

"What is that?"

"When?"

Paige smiled, turned her head so that she could kiss his neck softly, and then whispered the answer in his ear.

"Soon."

ACKNOWLEDGEMENTS

Many people helped bring this particular Paige MacKenzie story to life, and I owe sincere thanks to each one.

Heartfelt gratitude goes to Elizabeth Christy, whose top-notch editing keeps me on my toes. Her patience with my hectic schedule and panic over deadlines is commendable.

I owe special thanks to my brother, Jay Garner, not only for guiding me through the world of coin collecting, but for insightful advice on plot development through every draft of the book. If I ever find a cache of coins myself, I promise to share it with him.

Keri Knutson of Alchemy Book Covers created the fun cover concept for the entire Paige MacKenzie Mystery series, including the front cover of Hutchins Creek Cache. Leah Banicki is responsible for eBook formatting and full-cover layout. Tim Renfrow, at Book Design and More, deserves the credit for print formatting. Jay Garner, Karen Putnam, Carol Anderson provided essential beta reading. Louise Martens deserves extra praise for offering plot suggestions and listening to me chatter on and on for months about story development. As always, Carol Anderson also spruced the final manuscript up with her keen proofreading eye.

Above all, I am grateful for family, friends and readers who follow along with Paige and Jake's adventures, all the while providing support and encouragement.

CPSIA information can be obtained
at www.ICGtesting.com
Printed in the USA
FSHW01n2236080618
48928FS